Unsupervised

CORA KENBORN

Never settle for what's comfortable.
Go for what's impossible.
You just might surprise yourself.

Chapter One

LAKEN

Think back to your favorite rom com movie. Okay, now think about the turning point where the hero or heroine is broken, dejected, and thinks life can't get any worse. Maybe they look like they've been thrown down a wood chipper, or maybe they're pacing and mumbling to themselves, in need of a white jacket that ties in the back.

Good, now check me out. Yep, that's me sprawled out on my old, ripped, brown leather couch in a shredded evening gown with mascara running down my face like some circus clown reject. Don't judge until you've heard the whole story. I promise there's a reason for all of this, and I'm fully justified for the fucktastrophe you're currently witnessing.

My life is no rom com. I'm no heroine. I had it all in the palm of my hand and then my future went to shit, swirling down the proverbial toilet of life.

Overly dramatic? Stay with me.

Scooping an oversized spoonful of ice cream from the carton wedged between my knees, I shove it in my mouth and chase it with a few gulps of white wine straight out of the bottle. It has to be at least six a.m. on Sunday morning, and as I flip through the channels on the TV, those annoying rom coms I just spoke of mock me. Movies I used to devour, I now loathe and want to see die a slow death. Real life never wraps up in a pretty red bow at the end like they make you believe. No, it's messy, brutal, and rips your heart out only to pulverize it.

Tilting the wine bottle up again, I kick off my heels and settle on the movie *Titanic*.

Oh, good. A happy ending type of romance.

That's the way Shelby, my roommate, finds me as she swings the front door open to our tiny Bed-Stuy apartment in Brooklyn, staring at me as if I've been inhabited by some gluttonous alien. Shelby is a first-year medical intern with a crazy schedule and she's used to coming home at odd hours. What she's not used to is seeing me argue with a television screen.

"Holy shit!" Her hand flies to her mouth in a veiled attempt at hiding her shock. "Were you mugged? Oh God, did they follow you home? Do they know where we live? I have jewelry, you know."

Giving her a side-eyed glare, I lick the dripping ice cream off the spoon while choking the life out of the wine bottle. "Nope."

Walking farther into the room, she wrinkles her nose at my vices. "Then are you pregnant?"

"Piss off."

"Okay," she says, drawing the word out slowly. "Do you plan on going to work today, or are you just going to stay drunk until we're homeless?"

Let me stop here and remind everyone that I am neither drunk nor homeless. I've

3

lost my shitty job, but the fact of the matter is, that it's everything else I've lost that has caused this. And it's my own fault. A catastrophe of my own doing, like those contestants on *The Price Is Right* who bid four hundred and twenty-five dollars on a brand-new dining room set just to get on stage. They look so smug until the asshole next to them bids four hundred and twenty-six.

Seriously? Didn't they see that coming? The person next to them planned all along to make them feel secure in their win until it was time to turn the knife. Suddenly they're blocked in. Stuck. Screwed by their own stupidity, because Maude from New Hampshire doesn't give a shit about their feelings. Maude has an agenda and it's to screw them out of a new life...and a dining room.

I had everything. It was mine for the taking, and all I had to do was tell the truth. And I would've. I mean, I planned to... eventually.

Shelby stares at the hell hole I've turned

our apartment into and kicks a discarded Ho-Ho wrapper out of her way with the toe of her white sneaker. "Clean this shit up, Laken, then get a shower. You smell like fermented ass." Giving me one last eye roll, she stomps off to her bedroom and slams the door.

Taking another long swig from the bottle, I swish it around in my mouth before swallowing and calling out over my shoulder. "No, really, I'm fine. Just my life is ending, thanks for your concern."

And this is where my story begins. As a reluctant nanny to one of the most powerful families in New York City, I've waited for an opportunity like last night. All I needed was a chance to stick my foot in the corporate door. Once it fell into my lap, I latched on like a drowning woman on a life preserver. I met the executives I needed to meet, shook the hands I needed to shake, and integrated myself into a world I'd tried over two years to infiltrate. For once in my life, I almost had everything.

Like Leonardo DiCaprio, I was king of

my own stupid world.

That's the ironic thing about that movie, *Titanic*. Jack thought he had it all. He almost took a swan dive right over the bow of that boat like some lunatic while trying to save dumbass Rose. Not such a genius move. That should've been a clue to anyone watching that ol' Jack wasn't firing on all cylinders when it came to that red-haired chick, and things wouldn't end well. You know what? They didn't. Rose plopped her happy ass on that floating piece of wood while Jack's balls became little nutcicles and he froze to death.

You think that shit would've happened in real life? Hell no. Jack would've told Rose to scoot the fuck over, or he would've dumped her never-letting-go ass right in the North Atlantic.

Only the strong survive. Eat or be eaten. It's basic call of the wild, rule of the jungle protocol.

You probably think I'm the Jack in this story, right? That I'm at home pining away because I believed my soulmate loved me and didn't want me to die cold and alone at the bottom of the sea. You'd be partly right. But here's where you may not feel sorry for me.

I'm also the Rose.

Yep, I duped my Jack into thinking I'd share the piece of wood with him too. I made him care about the fake me—the one who didn't exist. All to get ahead in life. To get the prize I've always wanted. Until what I wanted was him.

I'm Laken Cavanaugh, and this is the story of how one unsupervised moment in Central Park started a chain of events that landed me at rock bottom, drinking six-dollar chardonnay straight from the bottle while stuffing my face full of chocolate ice cream.

Chocolate.

It's funny. I've always been a vanilla girl until I met him. In so many more ways than one. Now, I've lost my job, my career, my future, but most importantly, I've lost him. And it's all because of one little white lie. Well, a lie and the root of all evil. The bane of my existence. The reason why I'm one drink away from detox and a padded cell.

My boss.

Chapter Two
NIALL

Four Weeks Earlier

"I have no idea why the hell I'm here," I grumble and swipe a donut from the breakfast tray while dragging a chair out from underneath the far end of the conference table. Taking a seat, I tug on the tie knotted at the base of my throat. With every person who slaps me on the back and takes their seat, it tightens by the second.

I hate corporate America. I hate meetings. But mostly, I hate the way the woman directly across from me licks her red painted lips every time I catch her eye.

Slumping into the chair next to me, Vince pops open his briefcase and yawns for the third time since walking through the door.

"Stop being such an ungrateful prick. Look around, you're the only photographer in this meeting. This could be big for your career. Besides," he adds, smirking as he holds up a massive pastry. "Free eats!"

Taking a bite of my donut, I shake my head and wonder how a guy like Vince, whose idea of getting ahead means literally getting head, managed to climb the corporate ladder at Trask and Payne and not get slapped with a sexual harassment lawsuit.

"Ye know, there's more to life than food and sex."

"Sure there is." Inhaling half his pastry, Vince dismisses me with a wave of his hand. "I like a good nap in between a good fuck and a good meal."

I stare at him, and against my better judgment, push the issue. "The Ravenhill Gala Planning Committee has been in the works for months." I cast a quick glance around the table, taking in the faces of Trask and Payne's middle and upper management, along with their dutiful note-taking secretaries and figurehead board members.

"Everyone here has been in on this project from the get-go. Even ye slack arse has made an appearance when ye weren't hungover or balls deep in some intern."

"Damn, that's harsh, Niall." Vince manages to look offended for a full five seconds. "True, but harsh. Besides, I told you, at the last meeting, Gloria volunteered your Lucky Charms-eatin' ass to photograph the whole event."

"Do ye hear yeself? That's so politically incorrect, I don't even know where to begin."

He licks the icing off his lower lip and raises his coffee mug in the air. "Aye, she wants your shamrocks, man. She thinks they're magically delicious."

"Why do I hang out with ye?"

"Because without me, you'd spend your weekends painting nails and playing pin the tail on the donkey, and I don't mean the naked kind either."

I roll my eyes, making the mistake of glancing across the table. Gloria's stare is lethal as she enthusiastically licks the rim of her coffee mug for the second time in ten minutes. I have no idea what in the hell the woman hopes to accomplish. The move does nothing to entice me. In fact, with every swipe of her tongue, the coffee and donut I just scarfed down threaten to reappear all over the conference table.

With a low chuckle, Vince lowers his chin and makes the most disgusting kissing sounds I've ever had the misfortune of hearing.

"Shut your feckin' cakehole before I knock ye arse over tit," I mutter.

Lifting his own coffee mug to his mouth, he fights a smile. "I'm just saying, man, she sucks a hell of a dick."

"Ye had sex with her?" I stare horrified while catching Gloria's tongue making another pass around the rim of her mug out of the corner of my eye.

Vince sets his coffee down, his lips widening in that damn movie star grin that makes women fall at his feet. "Dude, most men at this table, and probably a few women, have fucked Gloria." Tilting his chin, he points them out, not giving a fuck who notices. "Bob, Frank, Todd…"

My mouth drops open, and I pin him with a blank stare. Mainly, because I have no bleedin' idea where the hell to go with that. "Christ…Todd? Are ye kidding me?"

Silence rings out across the table as all eyes turn toward Vince and me.

Feckin' hell. Okay, I didn't mean to say it that loud, but seriously, Todd? What was he thinking? Todd Reynolds is a family man. He has the life every man dreams of—a beautiful wife, two-point-five kids who get straight As and go to the perfect school, a house in the suburbs with a fence, and all the rest of that shite. Why would he risk it all to screw Gloria?

As if reading my mind, a low laugh rumbles in Vince's chest and he shakes his head at me. "Niall, don't be so sanctimonious. How do you think I got promoted to project manager? Hell, half the men in this room are only here because Gloria polished their knob." Eyeing me curiously, he fights a smirk. "Besides, you know she's going to collect sooner or later on getting Sophie into

Ravenhill. Might as well man up and take one for the team."

And there's the reminder of the day I sold my soul to the devil. Or in this case, the bitch of the board room. I wrote a contract in my own blood just to secure my daughter's future. One innocent inquiry into my kid's schooling ended up with me in debt to the black widow and no amount of financial reimbursement would get me out of it.

That woman wants to take it out in trade on her knees or her back.

Free tip for clueless parents: make sure to plan for ye kid's future at conception. As a single dad in New York City, no one told me that getting ye kid into the right school started at birth.

Seriously, am I the only person on Earth who had no clue this was a thing?

Apparently, it is in America. Only this shite begins with ensuring a kid is signed up for the right daycare, which progresses to the right preschool, which feeds into the kindergarten that farts rainbows and unicorns. I'm an Irish buck. When I moved to America and had a kid, no one told me everything I did from day one fecked said kid up for the rest of her life.

Vince kicks my chair as Mr. Navarro, the marketing director, stands and clears his throat. I struggle to pay attention and act like sitting in a business meeting and listening to a bunch of middle-aged men congratulate themselves on their worth is the best thing I've done all week. All I really want is to get outside and shed this suit. While I work for Trask and Payne Enterprises as a photographer, and don't get me wrong, I'm feckin' good at what I do, immersing myself in the culture of New York City is what I love. Being outdoors, experiencing life, and capturing nature as it happens centers me.

This pointless gathering is what my Ma used to call an opportunity for growth. I just call it shite that pays the bills.

"As you all know," Mr. Navarro says, pacing the room while patting his salt and pepper hair, "we only have four weeks left until the Ravenhill Charity Gala Dinner. Trask and Payne is sponsoring this event in a dual show of support for the children in our community as well as Gloria, our esteemed board member."

I sneak a glance at Gloria, whose bleach blonde hair is swept up into a twist and tucked with a clip at the nape of her neck. She catches me staring and attempts a coy smile. Instead of enticing me, it creeps me out. I feel like prey, and part of me is waiting for her to unhinge her jaw and slither across the table to swallow me whole.

"While most of you will be participating in the event in a professional capacity, we still expect you to attend in formal attire and socialize with our guests. We want to put our best face forward here at Trask and Payne, so keep the alcohol at a minimum, and please, no fraternizing with other employees. Are we clear this time, Vincent Tribiotti?"

Snickers ripple around the table as Vince shoots him a wounded look. "I have no idea what you're talking about, Mr. Navarro. I'm a perfect angel at these things."

The old man gives Vince a pinched smile. "Yes, well, if there are no further questions, we'll reconvene later in the week to begin final preparations. The gala is in four weeks, people, and it's going to be the talk of the town. Don't let me down on this." With a rap of his knuckles on the desk, he ends the meeting and walks out the door.

Vince Tribiotti could dive into a river of shite and come out smelling like a feckin' rose. That's just the type of buck he is. Not that either of us are saints. With the trouble that Vince and I have gotten into over the years, no one could ever accuse me of being a choir boy. However, I can't help but blame Vince for the shite hole I'm currently swimming in. It was his bright idea to get me hooked up with Gloria in the first place.

No, not in *that* way. Remember the donut? I'd prefer not to see it again, thanks.

Here's how I became a lost insect in the black widow's tangled web. Nobody warned me about that whole "plan from their birth" shite. When the time came for my daughter, Sophie, to go to school, I thought I could pick where I wanted her to go to school and make it happen because I'm not a complete feckin' dick.

Then my buddy Vince sold me out. The one guy I trust in this office set me up to be fecked, and not in the good way. For some reason, he has the goods on most everyone in the building. If ye want to know the dirt on anyone, ye go to Vince. He can tell ye who's sleeping with who, in what janitor's closet, and on what day. He's feckin' worse than a woman with new gossip.

Anyway, he found out that Gloria got around in more ways than one. In addition to being a Trask and Payne board member, she also sat on the board of trustees at Ravenhill Private School—the most prestigious primary school in Manhattan. They wouldn't even return my phone calls when I'd tried to get Sophie an interview. I'm a hard-arse by nature, but I'd do anything for my kid. Bitching to Vince over a few beers one night, led to him having a long chat with Gloria. It only took one phone call from her, and Sophie bypassed the interview and was placed directly in the school.

The power that woman possesses freaks

me out, I'm not going to lie.

Had I known then what I know now, I would've never blindly jumped into her web. There's an old Irish proverb that says, *the future is not set, there is no fate but what we make for ourselves.* Loosely translated, it means if ye are going to shite the bed, ye still have to lie in it.

Of course, I may be paraphrasing.

So, here I am, lying in my own shite bed, and the feckin' bitch has me trapped. Now she's watching me from the sidelines, biding her time until she can crawl over on her eight legs and devour me like the black widow she is. I should've known then that it would come back and bite me in the arse.

"I'm just saying," Vince reiterates, taking one last bite of his donut as he closes the clasp on his briefcase and drags it off the table. "You haven't gotten laid in a while. Gloria's no spring chicken, but there's something to be said for the age and experience of a hen who's been around a block fifty or sixty times." Slapping a hand on my back, he shoves the rest of the pastry inside his cheek and grins. "Think about it, Niall. She won't leave you alone until you pay her back. Might as well get it over with."

He's out the door and down the hall before I can think of a sufficient comeback, leaving me with the one woman no man should ever face alone unless he's wearing a cup.

Or five.

Gloria trails her fingers along the outer edge of the conference table with one hand, while wiping the lipstick from the corner of her mouth with the other. The tailored black business suit and red blouse she's wearing makes her look even more like her arachnid namesake. I have no idea what I'm in for, but judging by the hungry look on her face, it's nothing good.

"How is Sophie doing in school?" The question sounds innocent enough, but I've been around Gloria long enough to know every word out of her mouth is backed by an agenda. Besides, with my track record, I don't trust any woman as far as I can throw them.

"Grand," I answer, feeling my jaw clench as she closes the distance between us. "Cheers for the recommendation. She loves her teachers, her friends—"

"I just love helping children," she purrs, cutting me off mid-sentence.

Helping them, or baking them in an oven?

I have trust issues in general, but the minute Gloria mentions my eight-year-old daughter's name, warning bells go off in my head. The more I'm alone with her, the more I sense that Vince is right, and I'm about three seconds away from landing in the unemployment line.

It's not that Gloria is a troll. She's decent looking for an older woman, and if I met her in a bar and was desperate and drunk enough, I might even consider letting her get me off. At the end of the day, I'm still a man. However, I never shite where I sleep. Nothing good can come of mixing sex and work. Especially with a crazy bitch like her.

She sits on the conference table and crosses her long, toned legs. "The gala is getting closer, and there's still so much to do. I'm extremely humbled to be the guest of honor." Pressing her hand against her chest, she feigns shock, and I can't help but roll my eyes. A moment or two of silence passes between us before she leans back on her palms, appraising me. "You don't have to thank me for this opportunity, Niall."

I cock an eyebrow, irritation at being held hostage for a full five minutes now starting to overtake my good nature. "Thank ye?"

"For arranging for you to be the official photographer for the social event of the year. I know you haven't had a chance to thank me, but that's okay, I have a way you can make it up to me as well as for getting Sophie into Ravenhill."

"Make it up to ye? I was thinking a fruit basket would do the trick, to be honest, ma'am."

"It's Gloria," she corrects with a coy smile. "I'm not a woman who's afraid to demand what she wants, Niall. When I do favors for someone, I expect favors in return. Sometimes those favors benefit me professionally, sometimes they're of a more personal nature."

Shite. Here's where I lose my job.

"Personal nature?"

I'm an intelligent man. I was educated at Trinity College in Dublin, graduated with high marks, and consider myself to be gifted in both common sense as well as academics. However, for some reason, I'm standing there repeating everything she says like a feckin' parrot.

"An intimate nature," she clarifies.

I already know the answer, but something compels me to ask the question anyway. "Aren't ye married?"

Gloria slides off the desk and wraps her index finger around the tie I spent the entire meeting trying to prevent from choking me. Licking her lips, she tugs it forward and wraps it around her fist. "Technicality. We have an understanding. I understand his business ventures must come first, and he understands that I must come…repeatedly."

This feckin' bitch.

At first my heart sinks into the pit of my stomach. Then a hot blaze of irritation shoots through me. I'm about to shut this shite down right now.

"While I'm flattered, ma'am—"

"Gloria…"

"I'm not interested."

An unwelcome feeling pricks my skin. I've kept myself under the radar at Trask and Payne for two years. I'm the best photographer at this company, and I don't get involved in anyone's bullshite. I've prided myself in making my own way in this world and not bowing down to anyone. However, judging by the hard look in Gloria's eye, a moment of weakness ensuring my daughter had the best education has come back to bite me in the arse.

Her gaze briefly lowers to my zipper, and her mouth curves in a knowing smile. "It's a shame about the overcrowding problem at Ravenhill, don't you think?"

"What?"

"That's the thing about gifts, Niall. What's that phrase, easy come easy go?" Lifting a hand, she traces it along the waistband of my slacks.

I think I'm a relatively easygoing guy. Give me a pint of the black stuff, a good rugby match, and a regular piece of arse, and I'm a happy buck. I don't bother anyone, I don't start shite, and I'm not out to screw anyone over. However, start feckin' with my kid, and I'll become ye worst nightmare.

I smack her hand away from my belt with more force than necessary. "Are you threatening my daughter?"

"Correction," she says, raising a finger to emphasize her point. "I'm threatening your job *and* your daughter. One word from me and Sophie is kicked out of Ravenhill and learning addition next to juvenile delinquents. There won't be a damn thing you can do about it, either, because you'll be out on your ass peddling pictures in Central Park with a can and a cardboard sign."

I take a step back, staring into her cold green eyes. "Ye are bluffing."

Annoyance flashes across her face, and she laughs bitterly. "Am I? All I need to do is tell the headmaster that you falsified Sophie's records and then tell Navarro that you offered sex to keep me quiet when I found out about it. Everything you have will be gone in an instant, Niall."

"I didn't falsify anything and ye know it."

"Who do you think they're going to believe? A board member, or a second-rate photographer?"

"Why do ye even care?" I growl.

"I'm bored," she offers, dropping her eyes to my pants again. "And I want to know if your cock is as big as your sanctimonious Irish morals."

I should've just told her to eat shite and die. Maybe to also take the school and the job and shove them both up her aerobicized arse. But unfortunately, that's not what comes out. No, what comes out of my mouth is so much worse. So much more detrimental to my financial well-being.

"I'm engaged," I blurt out.

I have no idea what possessed me to say the words. I obviously had no forethought in the matter, or I'd have considered the fact that, eventually, I'll have to provide an actual living, breathing woman as proof.

And not the blow-up variety currently occupying Vince's bedroom.

"What?" she shrieks, pulling away and fisting her hands by her side.

"I'm engaged," I repeat, my delivery sounding more like a question than a statement.

Feckin' hell. Man up, Niall. If ye are going to sell this, stop being a pussy.

Gloria's jaw drops, but she quickly regains her composure, narrowing her eyes in suspicion. "When did this happen?"

"Recently." *Like two seconds ago.* "We met a couple of months ago. We've kept it low key."

Flattening her fire-engine-red lips, Gloria gives me a hardened laugh, straightens her spine, and runs a hand down the length of her suit jacket. "I think you're full of shit, Niall. I want to meet her. Bring her to the gala."

"That's in four weeks."

"Is that a problem?" she asks, raising an eyebrow.

Shite. I can't go back now.

"No."

"Very well, then. Oh, and, Niall?" Weaving her fingers through my hair, she digs her fingernails into the back of my head and stands on the toes of her red-soled heels. "Your fiancée is a lucky woman. I hope she knows that." Gloria scrapes her nails across my skin a little harder and then trails her hand down my chest.

Having had enough, I grab her wrist with enough force to let her know I'm done being fecked with. Jerking her arm, she dislodges my hold and with one last glare, she drags a pile of folders off the table and storms across the conference room without another word.

I let out a harsh breath. What the feckin' hell have I done? Of all the ridiculous things I've ever said, blurting out that I'm engaged may have just topped them all.

The minute Gloria storms out, Vince trails in after her, his eyes bouncing back and forth between us. "Dude, Gloria looks ready to kill someone."

"Vince, I need a date for the gala."

He grins and rubs his fingers together. "Now you're talking my language. I've got this under control. What kind of girl are you looking for—blonde, brunette, redhead, slutty?"

I rub my hands over my face and sigh. "The kind who'll agree to marry me in the next twenty-eight days."

Chapter Three
LAKEN

We regret to inform you that you have not made it to the second round of interviews for an internship with Trask & Payne Enterprises. While your skills are impressive, there were other candidates with qualifications more suited to our immediate needs. We encourage you to reapply in the future.

Increasing my pace across the snotty neighborhood in the Upper East Side of New York City, I crush the form letter in my hand and toss it into the nearest trashcan. Of course, I'll reapply. The five previous attempts were just a practice run for the main event. No sweat. Sixth time's the charm, right?

Wrong.

The sixth time will be a repeat performance of the epic failure that's my professional career. After four years of undergrad and two years of busting my ass in graduate school at NYU, it's obvious I'm doomed to live out the rest of my days as nanny to Satan's mistress. Even sucking up to Heather Trask's sister at NYU did nothing to help my climb up the corporate food chain.

Growing up, adults feed us all the same line of crap, and we fall victim to the biggest lie ever told.

You can be anything you want as long as you work for it.

Bullshit. I aced all the tests. I brought home all the medals. I was praised with all the honors, and where did it get me? Hoofing it up the steps to the most hateful bitch in Manhattan, that's where. All the pie in the sky ideals I'd been force-fed by the authority figures of my youth backfired when I graduated college and had nothing to show for all that hard work but a stack of rejection letters.

It's always the same song and dance. *You're overqualified, Miss Cavanaugh. You're underqualified, Miss Cavanaugh. You don't have enough experience, Miss Cavanaugh. You're wearing blue today, Miss Cavanaugh. You don't have a dick, Miss Cavanaugh.*

Okay, I might have made that last one up, but you get how unfair it is, right?

As I key in the code to the massive wrought iron gate leading to the estate I'd nicknamed Bitchtopia, I laugh at the sad irony of where my "so-called" career has dead-ended. I'm not particularly fond of children. I've never had any desire for my own. However, when I don't have my nose shoved in a book, I spend most of my time babysitting the kid from *Jerry McGuire*.

Okay, he's not *really* the kid from *Jerry McGuire*. That would be super creepy and a little disturbing considering that kid has to have a couple years on me, at least. He sure looks like him though. What the hell is that actor's name? Jonathan somebody?

And what a great movie line about her completing him.

Actually, I take that back. It isn't a great line. That line gives women unrealistic expectations of love and commitment. Screw you, Tom Cruise. Screw you and your meaningless bullshit. Renee Zellweger should've never fallen for that crap. The woman had a good, stable job with a respectable company, and just because old Tommy boy gave a rousing speech that stirred up her lady bits, she quit to work in a broom closet?

No, thank you.

I can't help my involuntary eye roll as I climb the marble steps leading to the front porch. *Front porch*? Do four-million-dollar homes even have front porches, or is there a some other pretentious name for them like podiatry landing plateaus?

Rich people are funny like that.

Thankfully, my eyes stop rolling before the door opens, and Lollie forces a tight smile of sympathetic camaraderie on me. That can only mean one thing.

Oh shit. Lady of Bitchtopia is home.

"Seriously?" Dropping my head back, I

sigh dramatically.

Lollie just nods, the corners of her eyes pulling down with worry as she wrings her hands over her crisp, gray maid uniform. "I tried to warn you, but you didn't answer your texts."

Since I sold my soul to the devil a year ago, Lollie has become a sounding board for my disdain of all things Hammerle. She shares my opinions, yet remains less vocal, happy for me to take the lead in the Lady Hammerle character roasts. She's a little skittish of any blowback, which I guess I understand considering she lives with the woman and depends on her for things like shelter and not being smothered in the middle of the night.

And can we please talk about the name "Lady Hammerle" for a minute? Who the hell decided she was a *Lady*? The woman has no blood ties to royalty whatsoever, and if she's British, I'm a Transformer.

I pat the canvas backpack on my shoulder. "Turned it off. I didn't want to deal with more inquiries from home."

Her face falls as she smooths the gray-streaked hair in her tightly pulled bun. "Oh, dear, another rejection?"

I start to roll my eyes again, something that's become a habit these days, when a shrill voice from inside the house carries through the foyer.

"Preston Bartholomew Kingsford Hammerle! What is this vile thing?"

I wince at hearing his full name.

Did she want him to get his ass kicked?

Preston's little six-year-old voice floats past my ears. "It's a butterfly rainbow, Mama. I made it for you."

She grunts, the loathing in her voice causing me to ball my fist on instinct. "Ugh, they're dead and disgusting. Get that thing away from me."

"But it's a present."

"Now, Preston! Don't test me."

"Yes, Mama."

I take in the little boy's crushed face and big, sad eyes hiding behind his thick Coke bottle glasses. His lip quivers as his small hand balls up a piece of paper boasting dozens of meticulously taped butterflies, just as I'd done with my own letter moments ago. Murderous thoughts fill my head as I shift my stare to the cold-hearted woman standing next to him sporting a well-honed bitch face.

I mentioned that I don't care for children. Well, most children. All except for Preston. I had one focus in taking this job, and it wasn't warm fuzzies from sticky-fingered hugs. Business is business. I wanted to stay detached, but I dare anyone not to love Preston. The kid reaches in and grabs your heart when you're not looking and rubs it all over his squishy little face.

"I think it's beautiful, Pres," I call out, hoping to erase his devastated frown. The moment he hears my voice, the corners of his eyes crinkle, and his lips lift into a wide grin.

"Butterflies," he states, as if that says it all.

And it does. To me, at least.

"Butterflies," I repeat, returning his smile.

However, blinding bleached teeth encased in fuck-me red lipstick ruin the moment. "Laken."

Mrs. Robinson, as I live and breathe.

"Lady Hammerle, I'm surprised to see you home."

And sober.

Glancing at her diamond-encrusted Rolex, she taps the crystal face and purses her inflated lips. "You're late."

"Only by a couple of minutes."

"A couple of anything in my world can mean thousands of dollars." Her judging gaze sears into me as I fight to control my temper. "Time is money, and money defines your time."

Too bad your time is spent underneath anyone other than your husband.

Unfaithful from her acrylic toenails to her platinum dyed roots, Mrs. Winston Hammerle is the walking, talking embodiment of a Stepford wife. According to Lollie, her favorite recreational activity is pole vaulting from one cock to the next in between her husband's European business trips. Refusing to grow old gracefully, it appears she thinks the fountain of youth comes directly from the tip of a twenty-year-old dick. Lollie has lost count of all the boy toys she's caught pulling out of the estate in the early mornings, sporting fresh scratches and the blank look of confusion.

"It seems you have issues managing both, darling."

Lollie shoots an arm out as I step forward, warning in her eyes. I push against her, inherently knowing my bank account and future need me to shut my mouth while my pride wants to force-feed her butterfly carcasses until she chokes.

I've lost my mind. It's the only logical explanation I can come up with for still being on her payroll. No, there's more to it. Mrs. Hammerle has connections at Trask and Payne Enterprises. A few years ago, she invested a couple million into the business and in return has the ears of executives. I need those ears, so I take her bullshit.

"You just have issues," I mumble under my breath.

Okay, I take it starting...*now*.

Lollie shakes her head as I offer her an apologetic grin.

"Grab your things, Preston," I call out. Reminding myself of the brass ring dangling at the end of this merry-go-round, I stifle the natural instinct to tell the *lady* of the house to shove this job straight up her ass.

Ushering him out the door, I mumble a half-hearted goodbye to Lollie and get us both the hell out of there. The entire trip to Central Park, I repeat the mantra I live by when dealing with that woman. If I want something bad enough, I can deal with just about anything to get it. Determination and success walk hand in hand with self-control.

I want an internship with Trask and Payne Enterprises. Lady Hammerle is my ticket through the door whether I like it or not.

The ends justify the means, and anything that happens in between is just a necessary casualty of war. All's fair in business and getting ahead.

Does that sound harsh? Probably, but

don't blame me. I don't make the rules.

But I'll damn sure play by them.

It has been ten months, one week, eight hours, twenty-one minutes, and seventeen seconds since I've had sex.

Not that I've kept track or anything.

Holy shit, has it been almost a year? No, that can't be right. Closing my eyes, I try to remember the last time my vag saw any kind of action that wasn't battery operated. His name was Kurt...or was it Kyle? Hell, maybe it was Kurt Kyle, I have no idea. All I remember about him is that he stuck his fingers inside me as if he were mining for gold and used phrases like "giddyup" and "boink." I don't care who you are, you can't respect a guy who growls that he's going to boink the fuck out of you.

But the guy I can't stop staring at? I'll bet money he's never used the word boink in his life. I'll bet my life savings—which currently stands at one hundred thirty-two dollars and sixty-eight cents—that his dirty bedroom talk would make my eyes roll back into my head.

He sits about twenty feet away from me at the western corner of Heckscher Playground, his chocolate brown hair sticking up every which way and dusting carelessly over his ears. A sexy as hell beard fills in his cheeks and skims his chin, giving off a clear rebel with a few worthy causes look. I usually go for the darker, brooding types, but something about the way the sunlight reflects off the strands makes him seem like a breath of fresh air.

That has to be the corniest thought I've ever had, and it makes me gag a little.

However, gagging doesn't stop me from forgetting all about cramming for my business law exam and concentrating more on the way his hunter green t-shirt clings to the muscles in his chest and strains against well-defined biceps.

He's alone, which is a plus. Trust me, I've watched him long enough to make the assumption. He also has a habit of licking his bottom lip, then biting down on his tongue when he stares at something. I wonder what it'd be like to kiss him? I bet he's a good kisser. Men who absentmindedly play with their lips and tongues usually know how to use them in other ways. The whole package is delicious and almost makes me ignore the fact he's holding a camera and taking pictures of little kids.

Oh. Well. *Ew.*

Perfect, pretty, and pervy. Two out of three don't win the race. Sorry, dude.

"Whatcha doing?" Knocked out of my lusty trance, my face flames as I refocus my attention on my entire reason for being in Central Park in the first place. Preston wrinkles up his red nose and sniffles as he pushes his falling glasses back up with a crooked finger. Springtime in the city is murder on a kid allergic to everything but sleep and water. With glassy, watery eyes, the poor kid looks like he's gone a couple rounds with a joint and lost.

"Studying," I answer with a groan.

He cocks his head and sneezes. "About

bugs? I can help."

"Bless you." He looks so serious that I can't help but ruffle his perfectly gelled hair. "Thanks for the offer, but this is more like statistics and due diligence laws."

He seems to mull it over. "A roach can live nine days without a head," he says after a long pause. "Did you know that?"

"Nope," I say, unable to hold the laughter in. He stares at me, blinking rapidly as if I'm a complete moron. "I wasn't aware, but I'll keep that in mind for my next beheading. Thanks, Pres."

His answering grin coaxes one of my own just before he sneezes again, spraying snot all over my textbook. "Laken, can I go play on the slide?"

I nod. "Stay where I can see you. I don't want you getting so popular that all the other kids fight over you." I give him a wink, and he rewards me with a wider smile.

"You're so silly." Giggling, he bounds off happily in search of his next big adventure.

Returning to the exam I'm destined to fail, ensuring my future as Lady Hammerle's foot soldier, I push tall, hot, and twisted out of my mind. My stomach churns as I remember the balled-up rejection letter, and I grip my pencil so hard I'm surprised it doesn't snap. My life may be on constant derail, but I still have a 4.0 GPA going for me. It's not much to hold on to, but if I play my cards right and stay on track, I could live out the rest of my days as the smartest, most frigid Waffle House waitress to ever flip a pancake.

I continue berating myself well into the third chapter of my text book when five solid years of my life are cut short. The minute Preston's congested cries for help hit my ears, I fling my pencil across the grass in a panic and scan the playground for his preppy vest and tailored khaki pants.

Because God forbid the kid is caught dead in a pair of shorts.

The moment I see him on the ground, my mouth drops open, and I take off in a full sprint toward the playground like my ass is on fire, swearing the whole time. Preston lay on his back in the sand, his glasses twisted and bent, fending off punches from another kid who's straddling him. The whole thing is like a scene from *The Sandlot* meets *Orange Is the New Black* as a group of elementary school kids crowd around them chanting and egging it on.

"Preston!" In a blind panic, I grab the bully's wrist and pull him off Preston's waist while the kid still is still throwing punches in the air like some tiny version of Rocky.

Hurried footsteps crowd in from behind. "Get ye hands off my daughter!" A defined, tanned arm snakes in from the side, scoops the brawler out of my grasp, and runs an attached hand down the boy's braided pigtail.

Oh, yum. Pervy guy has a hot accent. Scottish? Irish? Hell, he could be from Mars for all I care. As long as he keeps—

Wait. Backup—daughter?

Unable to process what has happened, I loosen my hold and step back, forcing my mind to focus on his words and not his delicious accent. "Your what?"

Pervy, hot accent guy with the camera hugs the bully kid to his chest, raising his eyebrows as if I just asked him to smell the number nine. "My daughter. Are ye finished manhandling my kid, for Christ's sake?" His last words trail off as he brushes a hand over her cheek. "Sophie, are ye all right?"

Fun fact for anyone paying attention. With me, mad equals verbal. Things fly out of my mouth with wild abandon that should probably stay tucked behind my lips. "Of course she's all right," I yell a little too loudly. "She was beating up Preston like a street thug."

Quirking his mouth, he gestures to her as if to imply I'm the stupidest being to ever breathe air. "Maybe ye missed the fact that she's a girl."

"Maybe you missed the fact that she could kick Mike Tyson's ass?"

"Maybe ye should've been paying attention instead of having ye nose in a book?" he counters, taking a step forward.

Fun fact number two about me. I like to argue. I'll argue about anything. You like apples? I like oranges. It doesn't matter if apples are really the nectar of the Gods, and I think orange juice tastes like a freshly squeezed asshole. If it's debatable, I'm debating it.

"You should try books sometime, or reading in general. Maybe you could start with consent forms for everyone to sign for all those pictures you've been taking instead of letting your kid run around unsupervised." Feeling smug, I point to his camera. "Or are they for your own personal enjoyment?"

See? Asshole juice.

His eyes narrow, little flecks of gold swirling in a sea of espresso. "Are ye calling me a pedophile?"

"Are you calling me negligent?"

A tug on the hem of my shirt breaks our stand-off as Preston sneezes and wipes his nose on the back of his hand. "I'm okay—"

"Stay out of it!" Pervy and I both yell at the same time.

Preston and Sophie back up, their little mouths rounding in matching Os. It's not until then that I notice everything has become deathly quiet. Managing a weak smile, I take in the crowd of onlookers who've gathered during my verbal volleyball match with the Ansel Adams protégé standing beside me.

Shit.

The name Laken Cavanaugh doesn't mean much in this city, but Preston Hammerle is a different story. The last thing I need is some trash magazine reporting that the Hammerle nanny let the heir apparent get the shit beat of him by a miniature Ronda Rousey while duking it out with her dad on the sidelines. I'll have to eat a little crow on this one.

But the brawler's dad beats me to it. Bending down, he holds the little girl's stare. "Sophie, did you hit this lad?"

She never flinches, her eyes steady on him and her tone flat. "Yes, I did."

"Why?"

"He went too slow on the slide," she says, cutting her eyes toward Preston. "Don't get up there and be a baby." With dark braids, pale skin, and the apathy of a serial killer, this girl reminds me more of Wednesday Addams than a normal kid.

Hot, foreign guy scrubs a hand down

his face and groans. "Soph…" Pursing his lips, he shifts his gaze to me, letting his amber eyes settle on my denim shorts before trailing them leisurely up my tank top to rest on my face. He seems to be appraising me, taking in every curve of my body and feature of my face.

An unfamiliar warmth spreads through my veins, and I swallow hard.

"Look," he nods to Preston while still holding my stare. "Sophie didn't mean any harm. Ye know how kids are, right? Why don't I buy ye both ice cream to make up for it?"

Preston's eyes light up like a megawatt microscope behind his glasses. "Please? I never get to have ice cream."

And this is how I get killed.

Because all crime documentaries begin with a young, single woman alone in a park with a strange guy taking pictures of her. She probably isn't even his kid. This is most likely a ruse to lure me into the back of a van.

"What do ye say?" he repeats with a wink. "That is, if ye are okay having ice cream with a reformed pedophile?"

Despite myself, I smile. "Double scoop with sprinkles and I won't call the cops. But don't press your luck."

Grinning a wide smile that crinkles the corners of his eyes, he nods to Sophie and tells her to collect their belongings. After bouncing her eyes back and forth between us, she narrows a warning stare at me and regretfully storms off toward the bench.

There are kids who just seem wise beyond their years—old souls trapped in a child's body. From her hostile reaction, I wonder how many actual souls she's killed, claimed, and trapped inside her.

With the two of us standing there awkwardly staring at each other, he finally extends an arm and holds his hand out by way of a formal greeting. "By the way, I'm Niall Mackay."

Don't tell him your name. Do not tell him your name.

"Laken Cavanaugh."

Shit.

"Don't worry, Laken," he says, giving

me a wink. "It's just chocolate ice cream. I don't pull out the chloroform and gags until the second date."

"Very cute. This is not a date; it's a peace offering," I assure him, taking a few steps toward the bench where I'd thrown everything to run after Preston. "And besides, I'm a vanilla kind of girl."

"Suit yourself." Collecting Sophie, he high-fives an overly-excited Preston and glances at me over his shoulder. "Oh, and about the chocolate? Never knock something until ye actually put it in ye mouth and taste it."

His words reignite the flush from earlier, and I feel my cheeks heat on impact. Images of what he'd look like underneath those tight jeans and t-shirt instantly dry my mouth and then make it water. Slinging my backpack over my shoulder, I grab Preston's hand and speed walk to catch up with him.

Slap my face on a milk carton…I'm in.

Chapter Four

NIALL

I stare at Laken Cavanaugh, the perfect woman who seems to be the answer to all my problems. Life doesn't work out this easily, does it?

Tucking her unruly hair behind one ear, Laken darts her tongue out as she tentatively licks the chocolate ice cream on her spoon. Within seconds her face scrunches up like she just sucked on a lemon.

"Still not a fan?" I ask with a chuckle.

She sips her soda and shrugs. "I'm just a creature of habit, I guess. I've stuck with vanilla so long, I don't see any reason to stray."

I can't help it. I wouldn't be me if I didn't mess with her.

Leaning forward, I flick a lock of her

golden hair away from her face. "So, are ye strictly vanilla in *all* things?" Heat crawls up Laken's neck, staining her cheeks a scarlet red. It's adorable, and I have an insatiable urge to run my tongue along the fringe of her blush.

"Are you always so forward with women you've just met, or is it just ones you plan on chloroforming?"

Grinning, I drop my spoon into the banana split bowl and grab the book sticking out of her open backpack. Giving the cover a once over, I raise an eyebrow across the table. "Business law? Do ye go to NYU?"

She nods, her long blonde hair falling over one shoulder. "Grad school, for now."

"That bad, huh?"

Shrugging, she wipes Preston's mouth with one hand while grabbing the book out of my hand with the other. "I'm a marketing major who has been trying to get an internship for over six months with no luck. It's just hard to see the finish line when everything is two steps forward one step back."

It couldn't be this simple, could it? She needs money and a foot in the door at a marketing firm. There has to be a way to finagle this girl an internship with Vince or Navarro in exchange for her help with Gloria. I have friends in some powerful positions. All the pieces are fitting.

"How so?" I ask, leaning in for emphasis.

"Well, I had to take a year off before college to..." she pauses, swallowing hard, "...take care of some things. Sometimes things happen in life you don't plan on."

A down on her luck, single mom, graduate student. This just gets better and better. My problem is about to solve itself. All I need to do is bait the hook and reel her in. Giving her a sympathetic smile, I nod. "Of all people, I can understand that."

She shakes her head as she licks her spoon. "I wasn't handed everything like most college students. I've worked for everything I have." Raising her blue eyes, she stares at me a moment before muttering under her breath. "I got enough financial aid to get me through undergrad because my mom is crazy and walked out on me."

Although I sympathize with her plight, I smile, thinking of my own free-spirited ma back in Ireland. "Most mothers are crazy."

She grimaces and looks down, not returning my smile. "No, my mom is actually crazy. I moved from Florida to New York City to literally start a new life."

"I'm sure ye think so, but—"

Laken swings a gaze back at me. "Have you ever heard of Whitesnake?"

"The eighties hair band?"

"Oh, so you're a fan?" She smirks.

I shrug and sit back in my chair. "I wouldn't say a fan, I just know of—"

Dropping her spoon, she folds her hands across the table and pins me without the slightest hint of amusement in her eyes. "You want to know why I'm alone in New York, making my own way? My pothead mother walked out on me to tour the country as a Whitesnake groupie along with my aunt."

"That's a joke, right?"

"Nope. She left me in the care of my senile grandmother for a life of head banging and random blow jobs." Sighing, she lifts a hand and swipes her hair out of her eyes. "I spent my childhood at the senior center overseeing Bingo games and eating dinner at four thirty because my mother found sucking on blunts and dicks more desirable than being a parent. Now do you think she's crazy?"

"I guess so." I nod toward Preston and smile as he and Sophie switch ice cream cones halfway through their own conversation. "Even with all that, he seems to have adjusted well."

Laken lifts her head, her eyebrows pulling together in confusion. "Who?"

"Preston."

Her forlorn expression changes the instant her eyes lands on him. Her mask cracks with obvious affection. "Oh, well, yeah. He's great. He's been through a lot."

She doesn't have to explain anymore to me. I get it, I've raised Sophie on my own for eight years since the ripe old age of twenty-two. My parents still live in Ireland, and while my Scottish grandparents have a brownstone in the city, they're well beyond retirement and too set in their own ways to help me care for her. While I love my daughter with all my heart, sometimes I wonder what life would've been like if I'd been able to live it as a normal twenty-something.

While other bucks my age spent their nights at bars and left with a different girl every night, I spent my nights at home with the same one who screamed bloody murder every time I stopped bouncing her. Other bucks had nameless women dropping to their knees and sucking their cocks. For the first year of Sophie's life, the only thing that got sucked around my apartment was my youth.

Not that being a dad stops me from getting my rocks off. I'm a father, but I'm still a man. A willing woman isn't hard to find. Sane women, well, that's a different story.

But this girl...

When I woke up this morning, I had two objectives; take some pictures to sell for some extra cash and try to figure out how to get the black widow off my arse—not necessarily in that order. The last thing I expected was for a solution to fall in my lap by way of my overly aggressive child.

And then Laken Cavanaugh happened.

I watched her behind the lens of my camera long before she saw me. I studied the way she chewed on her full lips as she read from her book, the way she twirled her long, curly blonde hair around her index finger, the little line that sank deep between her eyebrows when she concentrated extra hard, and the carefree laugh that lit up her face when she called out to her son. I wouldn't be a man if I hadn't also noticed the tight, little yellow T-shirt she wore and the cut-off denim shorts that showed off her long, tanned legs.

I spent a good half hour trying to figure out a way to talk to her. It had been a week since my conference room run-in with Gloria, and I was running out of time to ensure Sophie didn't get kicked out of Ravenhill, and my impetuous outburst didn't cost me my job. Luckily, my kid's temper finally worked for me instead of landing my arse in the headmaster's office, trying to explain why she pushed another kid.

Sophie isn't a bad kid, and I'm not a bad father. We've both just been through a feckin' ton of shite and are still trying to navigate our way through it all.

But back to Laken.

I'd spent all morning wracking my brain, trying to think of women who'd be possible candidates for my fake fiancée. My problem is that I have nothing to offer them in return except for me—and that's one offer I'm not willing to put on the table. No, I need someone who has something else to gain from this business deal. Someone who would agree to my terms, see the value for what it is, and then when the night is over walk away with a handshake.

That's why Laken Cavanaugh is perfect. She's just the type of date I need to keep Gloria off my back and my job safe. However, getting her to say yes to my outrageous offer is a different situation entirely. How does one proposition a woman into a fake engagement without getting smacked?

"Hi, so, I know my daughter just beat the shite out of ye son, but how about we pretend to be engaged for a night?"

The whole idea makes me look like an arsehole. What woman in their right mind would agree to that? I have a few dollars and an "in" at Trask and Payne. It's not a lot to sweeten the pot, but as long as she's into that sort of thing, it might work. It's not as if being on my arm is a fate worse than death. I'd be lying if I said I don't know I possess a certain appeal to women. American women are a sucker for a foreign accent, and being a native Irishman gets me more pussy than I know what do with.

I never go back for seconds, though. My choices don't just affect me, they affect Sophie. I have to be smart and keep my nocturnal activities casual and attachment-free. However, I need to approach this endeavor in a way that won't make Laken feel as though I'm buying her.

Which is exactly what I'm doing.

The perfect solution to my problem stares back at me with the most amazing blue eyes I've ever seen. Plus, the fact that Laken has a son makes her willingness to help me more probable. I have to appeal to her maternal instincts and make her an offer she can't refuse. One night is all I need to back up my story and make this whole mess go away. My job will be safe, Sophie's future will be secure, and maybe if I play my cards right, the night could even end with this girl on her knees.

Hey, a man can hope.

There's only one way to do this. If I don't come right out and ask, I'll never see her again. I may get slapped, or she may go for it. Either way, I have nothing to lose. Digging in my pocket, I hand Sophie a couple of dollar bills and tell her and Preston to go play video games. Laken eyes me curiously, as if she doesn't trust me.

Smart girl.

"So, how about ye let me make this whole thing with Sophie and Preston up to ye."

She motions toward the melted bowl of ice cream and smirks. "What do you mean?

Isn't this your grand apology? Fattening my ass with ice cream and whipped topping?"

Ye have no idea what else I could do with that whipped topping, Laken Cavanaugh.

I glance down to appear genuine. "Well, it's a start. But I'm thinking of appreciation on a larger scale."

"I'm listening."

I look up in time to see Laken twirl her tongue around the straw of her soda and all the blood in my body rushes south. Clearing my throat, I swallow hard and continue. "Well, ye mentioned that ye work a low-paying job, and ye are putting y'self through grad school, right?"

"Go on…"

"Well, it just so happens that I have this problem…"

She smacks the table with her palm and points a finger at me. "A catch. I knew it. There's always a catch. Is this where you whip out your camera and ask me to pose for a few pictures that'll never *ever* be posted on the internet?"

Cocking my head, I sigh heavily. "Are ye

going to listen or insult me?"

"Fine. Continue." Picking up her discarded spoon, she drags it through the melted mess in her bowl and takes a lick.

"Before I go on, ye aren't involved with anyone or have some abnormally large fiancé ye aren't telling me about, right?"

"I don't like where this is heading, Niall…"

"Just answer the question."

"No." She draws out the word slowly while pursing her lips

Exactly the answer I want to hear.

"Good. Do you want one?"

Laken blinks at me, the spoon dropping from her hand and clinking on the Formica table. "Excuse me?"

Giving her a wicked grin, I relay the story concerning Gloria and her indecent proposal, leaving out important details such as names just in case she tells me to go to hell.

An incredulous laugh breaks from her lips. "So, let me get this straight. You want me to attend a company party with you, pretend to be your fiancée, and then lie to your boss about it just so she'll leave your dick alone? Have I pretty much covered it?"

"No, smart-arse."

She raises an eyebrow.

"She's not my boss, but she could make my life hell. I just need her off my back."

Laken gives me an accusing stare, as if I have some grand scheme in choosing her. "Why me?"

Feckin' hell. Okay, I have a grand scheme, but that's beside the point.

"Why not?"

"That's not an answer," she argues, shaking her head. "What's in it for me?"

"Look, ye said ye need an internship, right? I have connections where I work, and I can get ye in front of people who make those decisions for my company." Frustrated this isn't going as easily as I'd hoped, I throw my hands up and slump into my chair. "Hell, I could ask a lot of other women and they'd do it just for the chance to walk into a Trask and Payne party."

Laken stills, her face paling. "I'm sorry,

did you say Trask and Payne?"

"Yeah, I'm one of their photographers, and for some reason, I also want to help ye. I think ye deserve a break." I let out a harsh breath and pack up to leave. "But if ye aren't interested, then—"

"Yes!" she screams, causing more than a couple of patrons to glance our way.

"Are ye sure ye don't want to think about it?"

"It's just one night, right? It shouldn't be that hard. A few hours of pretending to like each other won't kill me."

I scowl at her. "Ye are amazing for a buck's ego, ye know that?"

"So how do we do this?" she says, ignoring my jab. "Do we just meet there and make out on the dance floor?"

This going to be more work than I anticipated. "While ye make it sound quite enticing, it's a little more involved than that."

"How so?"

I study her for a moment. What we're doing is risky and walking into the lion's den unprepared is stupid. "Give me ye number. I think we should get to know each other a little. We need to be able to rattle off personal details about each other."

Laken sucks in a deep breath as if I just asked her to swim naked in a tank of starved piranhas. "You want to go out on a *date*?"

"Okay, we really need to work on ye not making that face every time ye think about spending time alone with me. It's kind of a dead giveaway." I squeeze the bridge of my nose in frustration. "Damn, Laken, have ye never played poker in ye life?"

"I'm a business major, Niall. Not a gambler."

"Ante up, Miss Cavanaugh. The stakes are about to be raised." Reaching into my pocket, I pull out my cell phone and punch in her name. "Now give me ye number."

After a moment's hesitation, she finally gives it to me, and I type that in as well. Once I hit enter, I follow it up with the call button and her phone rings. Raising an eyebrow, she digs it out of her backpack and answers.

"Hello?"

"This is Niall Mackay. Now ye have my

phone number. Program this shite in as My Big Dick Fiancé."

Laken wrinkles up her nose and makes a face. "You're disgusting."

"Aye, the loving way ye talk to me is why I fell in love with ye, my future fake wife."

Only a real man can handle pastel painted nails.

Don't question it. It's true. If ye see a man with Pure Baby Bliss #6 on one hand and Blue Mermaid Shimmer #9 on the other, don't question his masculinity. It takes a huge set of balls to carry that shite off.

That's exactly what I keep telling myself as I sit in front of the coffee table in our small Chinatown apartment as Sophie sticks her tongue out of the corner of her mouth and concentrates hard at turning my hands into feckin' cotton candy. I wanted to watch a movie. Sophie wanted to play dress-up.

Two guesses who won, and the first one

doesn't count.

"There," Sophie announces, blowing on my newly pink glittered thumbnail. "Don't move or you'll mess it up."

Right. Especially since that's the first damn thing I plan to do when she goes to bed.

Even hours later, the whole situation with Laken still seems too good to be true. While I'm not thrilled with the idea of introducing a woman I barely know to my bosses as someone I'm vowing to love and cherish till death do us part, this shite with Gloria leaves me no choice.

"Hey, Soph?" I ask, watching carefully as she closes the nail polish bottle. "What did you think of Laken?"

She tilts her head, drawing her eyebrows together. "Who?"

"Preston's ma. The lady from the ice cream shop."

She shrugs. "She's okay, I guess. Why? Are you going to marry her?"

"What?" Startled, I take in her wide brown eyes, a complete mirror image of my own. "No, why would ye say that?"

"You like her," she says matter-of-factly as she gathers her nail polish in a sparkly pink cosmetic bag. "When people like each other, they get married."

"Says who?"

"Oprah."

"Oprah, huh?" I rest my chin in my palm, making sure to keep my still wet thumbnail away from my face. "What happened to taking advice from more age appropriate women like Cinderella and that chick with fins. What's her name, Ariel?"

Sophie stands and pops her hands on her hips. "Daddy, honestly? Are Disney princesses really the role models you want for me?"

"Oh?" I ask, trying hard not to laugh. "We're revolting against princesses now?"

She rolls her eyes as if I should talk in grunts and walk around with my knuckles dragging the ground. "Ariel gave up her voice to run around on the beach after some dumb boy she barely knew, and he decided he loved her even though she couldn't even talk. This is the happily ever after you want for me?"

"Go to bed," I tell her, pointing down the hallway. "No more television for ye."

A half hour later, I sit staring at my phone mulling over either texting her tonight or waiting until tomorrow. I try to convince myself that my rush isn't about wanting to see or talk to her again, but more about wanting to get the logistics nailed down so when we arrive at the gala, there's no question as to how committed we are to each other. It has nothing to do with me wanting to hear her voice again. That would make me a spineless douchebag.

It also has absolutely nothing to do with the way she looked at me while licking the ice cream off that spoon, her clear blue eyes focused on me with inquisitive interest as I spoke.

Outwardly, she looks like the typical girl next door, but Laken Cavanaugh has a sarcastic streak a mile wide that entices me just as much as her incredibly tight body.

And that's saying something.

She's as American as apple pie, the Fourth of July, baseball, and the Star-Spangled Banner. The perfect American sweetheart to be the Irishman's fake fiancée. At least for one night.

I'm getting ahead of myself. My focus needs to stay on the prize. Less than twenty-four hours ago, I had no idea Laken Cavanaugh existed. This is a business arrangement that benefits both of us. That's it. End of story. The minute the gala is over, we'll part ways. If I can uphold my end of the bargain, I'll possibly see her around the office, and that will be that.

It has taken me eight years to get over the hell of Sophie's mother leaving us for money and the promise of a better life. The last thing I need is to think about someone else with the same ideals. Besides, I need to remind myself the only extra thing I want off Laken is a good time and an empty bed in the morning.

So why the hell can't I get her off my mind?

Chapter Five

LAKEN

At this point, all I can safely say about how I handled the situation is that I have some sort of deep-rooted death wish. The ability to stop myself from landing my ass in a whole lot of trouble rerouted from my brain to my mouth. It's the only way to explain walking away from Niall Mackay and not correcting him about Preston.

Being dick glamoured by way of a sexy Irish accent is no excuse for lying. That's exactly what you're thinking, and you're right, Even though we're concocting one big lie together in the first place.

But more on that in a minute.

After dropping Preston off on the Upper East Side of Manhattan, I make my way back home to Bed-Stuy after spending a good half hour arguing with Lady Hammerle over the ice cream stains on Preston's shirt. The only time the woman gives a flying shit about her son is when it benefits her to use him as a prop in public. She may have given birth to him, but she's no mother.

I can feel judgment here, and if eye rolling burned calories, you'd all be a size double zero. I know exactly what you're all thinking.

"Hey, Laken, if it's so bad, then quit. No one is forcing you to work for a bitch."

Watch Preston and his mother together for five minutes, and you'll know why I do it.

After realizing she'd be no help in getting my foot into Trask and Payne, I was fed up and ready to quit within the first couple of months. It was like trying to work a miracle with Heather Trask all over again at NYU, except at least Heather had been pleasant.

I even typed up my resignation letter and carried it with me every time I showed up at the estate to pick up Preston. But how do you walk away from a little boy who clings to you on his sixth birthday and tells you that his wish is for you to be his mom?

You don't.

Preston needs me, so I stay and avoid the bitch to the best of my ability. In a year and a half of working for the woman, I've had exactly four run-ins with her. Two of which have now happened in the same day.

Throwing my shit on the couch, I plop down and run a hand over my face. Why does the universe hate me? There's no good reason for doing what I did. Why in the hell did I let Niall think Preston was mine? Correcting him would've been so easy.

"While I'll agree to lie to the very people I'm trying to work for, Preston isn't my kid. I'm a twenty-four-year-old grad student, presently involved in the destruction of my own life."

What made me shut my mouth and pretend to be a struggling single mom while accepting the most asinine proposal of a lifetime? Who does that?

Me, that's who. He said the magic words that caught my attention and stomped my conscience into a pile of dust.

"Hell, I could ask a lot of other women and they'd do it just for the chance to walk into a Trask and Payne party."

Telling me he had a freezer full of blonde co-eds with big mouths would've shocked me less than knowing he worked for Trask and Payne.

Niall Mackay is my *in*. Five rejection letters would only lead to a sixth, and that bitch I work for would sooner wrestle in a cobra pit than help me. My only option left sat across from me, dangling an opportunity like a carrot.

Knowing what I'm about to do, I start rationalizing my actions. Sure, it's technically a lie of omission, but it's not like I'm willingly deceiving him, and it's not like he's a shining rose of innocence in all this. I never told him Preston was mine; he just assumed. It's his fault for assuming, right? I never actually verified his assumption, I just didn't deny it.

Technically, that isn't a full-blown lie. It's more like a lie-ette. You can't come back from a huge lie, but lie-ettes are explainable.

Besides, this isn't just about my career gains. Niall is getting something out of this charade too, and despite our unconventional meeting, I kind of like the guy. I'm interested in what he has to say, and not just listening to that sexy Irish accent—although I *really* wouldn't mind hearing it while horizontal and sweaty.

Hell, I don't even recognize myself around him. I smile. I lean into him. I bat my freaking eyelashes. When was last time I batted anything at anyone? Did I even do it right, or did he think I'd lost a contact lens?

No, this is wrong.

I squeeze the life out of my phone, staring at it like it has all the answers in the world. I know it's wrong. A decent person would call him, blurt out the truth, cancel the date, and then change their number.

That's brave, right? Certainly not the chickenshit way out.

But if he only knew how hard I'd worked—how one word from someone on the inside could change the rest of my life—he'd understand. He seems sympathetic to my plight as a single mom, and this ruse of ours hurts no one.

Honestly, where's the harm in it?

I know I'm not *really* a single mom. There's no plight. Okay, there's a plight, but it's me and my aversion to panhandling for crusts of bread.

I sit and mull it all over. The longer I hold my phone, the more I know what I need to do. I've waited too damn long for this and worked too hard to ignore an opportunity when it falls into my lap.

I'm going to accept the invitation to attend a Trask and Payne gala with Niall Mackay as his fiancée. It's a win-win. Niall needs me on his arm to keep the vulture lady away, and I need to be on his arm to get a foot in the door to my future. I'll figure out the rest along the way.

I hope.

The next morning, I stare at the text, my toothbrush hanging out of my mouth as toothpaste foams around my lips.

My Big Dick Fiancé: To make this look good, we should get to know each other a little better. What do you say we go out just the two of us? No kids.

This is where life throws a curveball I don't expect. I know I willingly gave Niall my number, so, logically, the fact that he followed up with a text shouldn't shock me. However, I'm still wrapping my head around the idea that I'm now someone's fake fiancée. Nobody said anything about dates. And without kids? Forget it, Preston is my safety net.

Rinsing out my mouth in the bathroom sink, I wrap my long, curly hair into a messy bun on top of my head and secure it with a clip. I need reinforcements, but, unfortunately, only one person comes to mind. With my heart pounding in my chest, I tear down the hallway, screaming for Shelby at the top of my lungs.

I barely turn the corner when her bedroom door flies open and she stands in the doorway, one palm braced against the frame and the other holding a lamp like a sword. Her matted shoulder-length red hair is matted and sticks to her lips as her eyes widen and scan the room for something to smash.

"What? Fuck, is someone in the apartment? Are you hurt? Don't just stand there, Laken! For God's sake, get the phone and call the cops!"

"Huh? No, it's him." I hold up my phone as if that explains everything.

Shelby lowers the lamp, raking her hair out of her face as she blinks at me. "Who's him?"

"I got a text."

"Is it about the murder?"

I toss her a confused look. "There was no murder."

"There's going to be," she growls, her face darkening.

In the three years Shelby and I have lived together, she' has always been the level head to my neurotic. Our friendship is contractual. I pay half the rent and so does she, ensuring we both don't sleep on a bench in Central Park. Shelby usually doesn't have time for things like girl talk, smiling, or pleasantness in general. We've never been particularly close, and she never misses an opportunity to point out my flair for the dramatic. However, I need to confide in someone outside the situation who'll give it to me straight.

"I have a problem."

"Shocker."

"I'm serious, Shelby."

"You have five minutes."

"Does renting myself out make me a whore?" I ask, chewing my cheek.

Replacing the lamp, she rests her hands on her hips and sighs. "Laken? What the hell have you been doing while I'm at work?"

Bracing for her reaction, I squint one eye and let it rip. "I'm engaged."

She reaches for my left hand, and after finding my ring finger bare, she tilts her head to the side. "Come again?"

Shelby listens quietly as I relay the entire story from the park. She nods at certain parts and raises an eyebrow when I show her

Niall's texts and she sees his contact name is *My Big Dick Fiancé*.

When I finish, I take a huge breath and throw my hands out to the side. "Well?"

"This is going to backfire on you, Laken. Lying is never a good idea. Eventually that shit comes back to haunt you."

"I know," I admit.

"But still," she says thoughtfully. "It's an in with Trask and Payne, and God knows you're never getting an interview by yourself."

"Your confidence in me is astounding, thanks."

"Well, it's not like the guy is a creep, right? He has a kid. That has to count for something."

"Sure, I mean, we shared a few stories, and I managed to not end up a missing person on the evening news." Pressing my thumbs against my temples, I frantically pace the room. "But I don't know him. Shelby. He could still be a homicidal killer hell bent on stuffing me down a well and making a woman suit out of my skin."

She rolls her eyes and shoves past me into the living room. "You've been watching *Silence of The Lambs* again, haven't you?"

I wave a hand, dismissing her. "That's beside the point."

"Okay, you agreed to this fake fiancée crap, and this is your chance to get in with Trask and Payne." Flouncing onto the couch, she props her feet up on the coffee table. "You're not actually marrying the guy. What are you really scared of?"

"I don't know. Yesterday it seemed like a good idea, but today…I don't know."

"He's not really roping you into the whole 'till death do you part' stuff, you know that, right?" she offers as I sit down beside her and throw my head against the back of the couch. "Besides, he sounds like a hot guy with a good job. How bad can he be? The man just wants to get your stories straight, and from the sound of it, you need to get laid more than you need to worry about the consequences of what you've already agreed to." Grabbing the remote control, she turns on the television, ending our conversation by pressing the volume button until I can barely hear myself think.

With my phone in my hand, I think about what she said and it starts to make sense. What exactly do I have to lose? All I need to do is get to know the guy and lie to my future employers that I'm head over heels in love with him.

Piece of cake.

Besides, if there's a little side action along the way, that's just a bonus.

As some talk show host rambles on at a decibel about to shatter my eardrum, I text Niall back and hold my breath as I hit send.

No kids—no fiancée. What kind of woman do you think I am? You think you can just put a ring on my finger and I'm that easy? Oh, wait. That's right. You didn't. Meet me at Heckscher again at noon—with Sophie.

His response is immediate.

My Big Dick Fiancé: I don't know; **are** *you that easy? Might be fun finding out for myself. Keep up that smart mouth and you can forget about a honeymoon in Mexico.*

Oh, and since we're throwing out demands, make it near the island at Turtle Pond at one p.m. Love, your Big Dick Fiancé.

I let out a scream and throw my phone across the room, because although I'm pissed at him, I know for a fact I'll be there promptly at 12:55.

With Preston in tow, I show up at 12:45, hoping to scope out a spot and watch him as he arrives. The area of Turtle Pond he selected is a bit secluded, and it makes me wonder if he chose this location for the ease of hauling me off in the van I still imagine he has.

I mean, let's be honest. I don't know the guy. If I'm getting myself into this farce, I need to know exactly what kind of man I'm tangling with. This is purely an information-gathering venture. It has nothing to do with wanting to watch the way his muscular body moves with the ease of a man who knows his worth, or the way his mouth quirks up in a crooked smile every time he mentions the word fiancée. And it's especially not the way his sexy Irish accent just rolls off his tongue.

Shading my eyes from the sun, I glance around and finding no sign of him, I decide to get comfortable while I wait. Completely focused on spreading out the quilt so Preston can play with his action figures, I don't hear him sneak up behind me.

"Daydreaming again? I wouldn't make a habit of that in public places, Laken. Anyone can just walk up and take advantage of ye."

Letting out a yelp, I twist around so fast I fall on my ass. I know I have that guilty look in my eyes. You know, like when your roommate knocks on your door seconds before you turn off your Magic Wand vibrator.

Oh, that shit happened to me late last night after having a particularly animated and detailed dream about Niall. I tried to mask the chainsaw sound, but it's kind of hard to do when you have the most archaic vibrator from 1972 burning your clit off. Okay, honestly, this thing isn't even a real vibrator and probably needs to be retired, but I'm not one to just walk my ass into a sex toy store and peruse the aisles like I'm buying fertilizer at Walmart. However, after Shelby narrowed her eyes this morning and asked me if I'd successfully chiseled my way to China, maybe I'll do some online shopping and see what I can find.

Muscles twitch in my jaw as I stare up at him. "Take advantage of me, huh? Present company definitely excluded."

He grins and heaves a long sigh as he extends an arm and hands me one of two half-melted chocolate ice cream cups. "Again, ye need to work on pretending to like me, Laken. If not, the woman we're trying to convince is going to see straight through ye."

"Chocolate?" I ask, lifting an eyebrow at the frozen concoction.

"Just keep licking." His grin widens along with the blatant innuendo. "Ye learn to appreciate the taste." The wind picks up, blowing through his messy hair. He runs his fingers through it and then offers me his

86

hand.

Holy fuck.

Okay, time out for a minute. Back to my rom com fetish. There's a point in the movie where the heroine suddenly sees the hero and a burst of sunlight erupts from the back of her head while cheesy music starts playing in the background. This is the viewer's clue that this poor dumb girl has finally realized that the geeky guy she's been palling around with for half of her life isn't so geeky. He's got muscles on top of rippling muscles and a ten-inch cock that seems to have grown overnight.

You feel me?

Well, I've only known Niall Mackay a day and a half, but cue the cymbals and drums because even though I have no business gawking at him the way I am, he looks too delicious not to fully appreciate. Dressed in khaki cargo shorts, a white graphic t-shirt with what I assume to be some intricate Irish crest on the front, and tan boat shoes, the whole outfit seems casual yet somehow hotter than if he sported a three-piece suit with a designer power tie.

This is the moment I realize how much trouble I'm in with this so-called arrangement of ours. While I've prided myself for six years on being able to keep my eye on the prize and maintain a strategy of not getting hung up on any guy longer than it takes to sneak out of his bed in the middle of the night, Niall Mackay is blowing said strategy all to hell.

I accept his hand, and as Sophie and Preston make their way to the water's edge, Niall lifts a paper bag, smirking at my less than enthused expression. "Are ye ready for some intense family bonding?"

"Is this where you break out the chloroform and we find one of our very own to kidnap?"

"Ye are never going to let that one go, are ye? No, I thought we could have some fun with the kids and race some paper boats while we go over some points that might come up at the gala. Ye do remember the whole reason for our hanging out today, right?"

"Of course, I do," I snap, trying as best as I can not to focus on the way his forearms ripple as he grips the handle of the bag. "Paper boats?"

"Wow, ye really are a city girl, aren't ye?" He grins, pinning me with the sexiest smile I've ever laid eyes on. When I continue to stare at him in that *get to the point* way, he pulls out a shitload of newspaper, duct tape, and a handful of different colored Sharpies and points toward the water. "I'll handle the construction, and ye man the decorating station. We're going to make paper boats out of this shite and race them in the water."

"Can't we just let the kids play while we hash this out?"

Light flickers in his eyes, and he looks like he's trying not to laugh at me. "Why? Are ye scared I'll win?"

Did you catch that? I did too, and although my rational side tells me he's baiting me, the other side—the one that can't seem to back away from a challenge no matter how small my chance of winning may be—fist pumps the air like Judd Nelson at the end of *The Breakfast Club* and dives in headfirst.

Grabbing the Sharpies out of his hand, I hold them like a machete. "I'm scared you'll embarrass yourself and cry like a little girl when you lose, yes."

"Okay…" He draws out the word and stares at me like he's trying hard to figure out my angle. "I like a confident woman. Care to make it interesting?"

"How so?"

"If your boat wins, I'll get ye an interview with my friend, Vince, *before* the gala."

Hello, offer I can't refuse.

"Keep talking, I'm liking these terms." Then the alternative hits me. "Wait, on the off chance that a miracle occurs, what happens if your boat wins?"

His head turns, and his heated brown eyes find mine, ensnaring them in a hold I can't look away from. "Ye have to kiss me. And, what's more? Ye have to feckin' like it."

Somehow the thought of kissing him overrides my good sense, and before I know what I'm doing, my head bobs up and down like it's not even attached to my neck.

"Then it's settled," he says, sealing the deal with a final nod and turning his attention toward the project at hand.

I shouldn't be amazed that Niall is somewhat crafty. He's a photographer, and artistry certainly runs in his blood. However, as we all sit on the blanket, I observe his patience with Sophie and Preston with awe. It's mesmerizing to watch, and a strange warmth fills my chest as he shows them step by step how to expertly fold the newspaper to form the boat, ensuring it floats. Suddenly, he's not just the outrageously hot guy who offered me the deal of a lifetime. He's a real person. He's a father. He's someone I could see a woman easily falling for.

Even me.

As the kids squeal and run off holding their new boats like their most prized possession, Niall turns to me. "Let's get some basics out of the way."

"Like my middle name and where I'm from?"

"Well, I was thinking more like whether

you sleep in lingerie or nothing at all."

I stare at him in shock, my thinly held self-control starting to crack. "Are you always this forward?"

"Aye," he says, flashing that damn adorable smirk that makes me forget why the hell I'm mad in the first place. "But mainly, I like making ye cheeks turn that beautiful shade of red."

I lower my chin to my chest. "I don't blush."

"Oh, ye blush, all right." Amusement creases the corners of his eyes. "Do I make ye nervous, Laken?"

"Paige."

"Excuse me?"

"My middle name is Paige, and I grew up in a little town right outside of Boca Raton, Florida." Standing, I dust off the grass stuck to the back of my legs and nod toward the water. "And if the inquisition about my nocturnal habits is over, we have two antsy kids almost as anxious to kick your ass as I am. Is the fleet ready to set sail?"

Gathering the makeshift boats in his

arms, he calls out after me. "What about the sleepwear?"

Pausing halfway to the water, I toss a grin over my shoulder. "Full flannel pajamas."

Which is a lie. I sleep in the nude. A small part of me hopes maybe someday soon, he'll find out for himself.

Forty-five minutes and twelve boats later, all three of Niall's paper armada sail flawlessly across the water while one of mine is resting in a watery grave at the bottom of the pond, another is floating upside down, and the third is hung up on some overgrown grass by the bank. As much as I've lusted over the man in the past twenty-four hours, and almost set fire to my own vagina trying to masturbate him off my mind, the idea of conceding to him isn't high on my priority list.

Standing by the water's edge, I contemplate taking a swim to save my last hope at winning this bet, when I feel warm breath on my neck.

"Looks like ye got y'self in quite the situation here."

"Nope," I say, popping the P at the end as I poke my boat with a stick in hopes of dislodging it. "All under control."

Tightening my grip around the useless stick, the only control I manage to have is pushing the shit further into the brush, causing it to tip over and take on enough water to sink. I curse and stomp my foot, spraying water and dousing the top of the newspaper. As the tip of my boat shoots up, it bobs haphazardly for a moment, then begins to capsize under the murky water.

"Piece of shit boat!" I scream and blow a wet piece of hair out of my eyes, frantically jabbing the stick harder as I wade farther into the water.

Niall peers over my shoulder again. "Need some help?"

"Stay out of this," I growl, still determined not to lose. "Did you sabotage my boat to win this bet? Can't you get a girl to kiss you without cheating?"

"Look, if ye just let me help ye—"

"I. Do. Not. Need. Help."

I know I look like a drowned rat. I'm

half drenched, chasing after a stupid boat so I don't have to kiss a man who I desperately want to kiss. Makes zero sense, right? However, what the hell am I supposed to do? There's no wrong answer to this equation. If I lose, I get what's probably the most amazing kiss of my life, and if I win, I get the chance for an in at Trask and Payne without doing jack shit to earn it.

So, you tell me. What would *you* do?

Know what you probably wouldn't do? Distract yourself while jabbing a stick over a pond on your tiptoes. As I'm mulling this over in my head, the boat finally dislodges the minute I decide to give it one last Herculean jab. You see where I'm going with this, right? There's only one way this can end, and it's right in the middle of Turtle Pond.

With one slip of my cute sandal, I dive headfirst into the water. It's not one of those graceful, "oopsie" moments either. No, this is a mouthful of dirty-ass pond water, hair in my face, and pond scum now coating my skin, type of swan dive.

The minute I catch my breath, all I hear is Niall's hysterical laughter in the background. Between holding his stomach and wiping his eyes, he manages to check on my well-being. "Are ye all right?"

Embarrassed, I cross my arms over my chest. "If you're finished being an asshole, you could give me a hand, you know."

When he extends his hand, I do what any female in my situation would do. I plant my feet and use the resistance of the water as leverage, giving his arm a firm tug. I can't help the feeling of satisfaction when his eyes widen with shock right before he tumbles headfirst into the water right beside me.

The minute his head pops up, I'm prepared for him to tell me to go to hell, or even worse, that the deal is off and I'm right back to sending out worthless internship requests.

Instead, he wipes the water from his face and takes a few steps toward me, his eyes gleaming. "Well played."

I force a smile. "Niall, look at you. You're all wet behind the ears."

"And ye lost a bet."

"Well," I say, beginning to make my way toward the shore. "I suppose we can talk about payment when—"

In two steps, the water parts, and Niall gathers me in his arms. All the breath leaves me in one swoosh as his lips find mine, and the cool water evaporates only to be replaced by blazing fire. The kiss starts out soft as he traces the seam of my lips with his tongue, his hands dipping to the base of my spine and pulling me flush against his wet body. A soft moan escapes my lips before I can rein it in, and the minute I embrace him back, he deepens the kiss so fiercely I can barely breathe.

This kind of kiss scares me because I can get lost in it, and in the end, this is a contract—a one-night arrangement that benefits both of us. Besides, I've somehow let the man think I'm a single mother in need of rescuing. The game is already in play. It's too late to change the rules now.

If everything goes as planned, Niall and I will be co-workers soon. If I'm ever to be respected as a professional, this can never happen again. Even if it's physically painful how much I want to keep kissing him.

Pulling away, I nod toward the blanket where Sophie and Preston laugh and demolish their soggy boats, oblivious to what just happened between us. Extending my hand, I offer a weak smile. "Congratulations on your win, Mr. Mackay. Don't expect it to happen again."

Making a show of wiping our kiss from his bottom lip, he eventually shakes my hand and winks. "Oh, I expect that and a lot more, Miss Cavanaugh. Count on it.

Chapter Six

NIALL

"Have you kissed her yet?" Sophie purses her lips and glances up with a knowing look.

When the hell did this kid turn into an adult? And when did she start paying enough attention to know Laken isn't just one of the regular playdates I usually drag her to?

"No, and it's none of ye business." I try to fix the mess I've made of her hair before school. Dragging a brush through the rat's nest, I again attempt what should be pigtails, but ends up looking like one cheesed-off donkey humping another one.

Completely ignoring me, she winces as I pull the elastic bands tighter and give up. "Are you gonna kiss her?"

That's the million-dollar question. When I kissed her at Turtle Pond, something changed between us. Now, almost four weeks later, we've seen each other almost every weekend, spending time with the kids at Central Park Zoo, a day trip to Coney Island, the Children's Museum…hell, almost everything *but* spending time alone. Not that she hasn't been giving me some serious signals. With purposeful touches, lingering caresses, and her outfits getting tighter and skimpier, something needs to give. At the end of the day, I'm still just a man.

Plus, I'm starting to get callouses from jerking off all the time, and I'm going to go broke paying my water bill from all the cold showers.

We've already learned the basics about each other, enough to not look like feckin' liars if someone questions our union, but Laken is still holding back. It's almost as if she's afraid to let me see the real her—like there's something she doesn't want me to know. It irritates me, because I've let her into my world more than I've allowed any other woman since Sophie's mother wrecked my trust.

"I don't know, Soph. Why are we even talking about this?"

"Because you like her."

That's beside the point.

Dropping the brush, I chuckle and scratch my head with my index finger. "When did ye become an expert in anything but Oprah and being mad at the world?"

"I like Preston," she says with a blank expression.

Sophie has always been a master at schooling her emotions. It freaks out adults, and as abrasive as she is, I used to think I was doing something wrong. Eventually, I realized it's just in her genes. She's one of a kind and marches to the beat of her own drummer. Kind of like her father.

I raise an eyebrow. "Ye do?"

"Well, not in the beginning," she admits. "But he's not so bad. I like Laken too. You should marry her."

"Ye think so, huh?"

Chewing her thumbnail, she thinks for a

moment. "Tomorrow works for me. I'll wear a dress, but no shiny shoes. I like sneakers."

"Nobody is getting married, Soph."

A hint of a smile crosses her lips. "That's what you think." Bounding down the hallway of our small apartment, she stops at her bedroom door and turns over her shoulder with a wink. "Don't worry, Dad. I've got this under control." With a maniacal laugh, she throws her head back and disappears into her room while slamming the door.

Oh, feckin' hell, this can't be good.

Sophie has never been a conventional child. Spirited and unique is what her teachers tend to call her. I'm not sure what that's supposed to translate to, but I'm thinking they probably get together, down a few tequila shots, and draw straws to see who ends up with the Mackay kid the following year.

Is that horrible to say about one's own child?

However, Sophie is right about one thing. I *do* want to kiss Laken again. If I close my eyes, I can still smell her jasmine perfume and hear her throaty laughter from the pond. Just thinking about the way she looked dripping wet, with her clothes stuck to every curve, warms my skin. Her body is amazing, and the more we're together, the more I imagine what it would feel like underneath me all slick and wet as I thrust into it. Would she scream my name or moan softly in my ear as she came?

This definitely isn't good.

Reaching down to adjust my inconvenient erection, I try to think of anything but Laken. I'm not supposed to want her, and the fact that this is just an arrangement of convenience makes me crave her even more. Maybe it's that whole forbidden fruit thing. Maybe wanting what I can't have makes her seem way more enticing than she is?

Then I remember the heat in her eyes when I tried to pull her out of the water. This is new territory for me. I've never had to work so feckin' hard for a woman's attention. Normally, they throw themselves at me and I have my choice of which one I want for the night. The fact that it has taken so long for Laken to warm up to me pisses me off and entices me at the same time. What kind of mental bullshite is that?

It's clear to me that I won't be able to get over her until I'm balls deep inside her.

That settles it. I'm fucking Laken Cavanaugh.

I stare at my cell phone sitting innocently on the coffee table. I've put it off, but the simple arrangement I thought I had under control has turned out way more complicated than I imagined. I've kept this whole charade to myself for weeks, but maybe enlisting some help isn't such a bad idea.

Besides, who better to help me sleep with a future Trask and Payne employee than a buck who's fucked probably half of the females in the building? Swiping my phone off the table, I fight a yawn as I punch in the number I know by heart.

Vince answers on the first ring. "What's up, dickhead? Where the hell are you?" His voice is muffled by clanging and chatter in the background. "Please tell me you've decided to tickle Gloria's happy button because she's especially bitchy this morning."

Vince Tribiotti is about as subtle as a sledgehammer.

"Not happening. Get over it."

However, he refuses to give up the fight. "You know you'd be making everyone's lives more bearable, right? I mean, this is worse than the shittiest case of PMS I've ever had the misfortune of witnessing."

"I'd rather get my dick caught in the ceiling fan."

The unmistakable sound of air sucking through clenched teeth fills the line, and Vince groans low in his throat. "Quit it with the dick threats. I don't care if it is just your pathetic shriveled up piece of meat on the line."

This conversation is headed nowhere fast, and I'm already late for a meeting with Sophie's teacher. I pour another cup of coffee and cut to the chase. "Look, I need to go, but are ye free for lunch today? I need ye opinion on something."

"Not today, man, but it doesn't matter because I need you and your camera-toting ass at the office as soon as you can get here. I've got a campaign I need you on."

I tilt my head down the hallway to make sure Sophie's door is still closed before answering. "I took today off for some bullshite teacher conference. I can't bail on it." Although I'd love nothing more than to bail. Even to fight off Gloria and her twelve hands.

"Non-negotiable," he says, a smug edge to his tone. "Have your ass on Madison Avenue in an hour. Don't fucking let me down on this, Mackay, or I'll kick your ass."

Taking one more gulp of coffee, I grumble and pour the rest down the drain. As much as I want to help out my friend, the last place I want to be is anywhere in Gloria's grabbing distance. "Can't ye get someone else?"

"No can do. You were specifically requested. I'm just following orders."

I sigh and scrub my hand down my face. "Can ye at least take me out for dinner before ye screw me over next time?"

"Be here in an hour."

"An hour and a half, and ye better have

a shite load of coffee."

Vince mentioned Gloria, and I made a decision. Why wait until the gala to start showing off my new fiancée? Three weeks of planning has been more than enough preparation to present the lie Laken and I have concocted.

I'll admit to having somewhat of an agenda when I concoct a plan to invite Laken to meet me at the office, and I hope it doesn't backfire on me. But, this is Laken Cavanaugh we're talking about, and nothing she does should surprise me by now.

After cutting my meeting short at Sophie's school, I text Laken and tell her to meet me at Trask and Payne. I fully expect some sort of argument from her, demanding to know why and wanting a play-by-play account of what to expect. However, to my surprise, barely a few seconds go by before a return text pops up with a "yes" followed by seven exclamation marks. Seven seems a little excessive, but I think maybe she's getting into this engagement ruse as much as I am, which gives me hope.

The project Vince mentioned ends up with me alone in a conference room, taking publicity shots of Gloria. It's for some society page only rich people read that's promoting the gala and her ability to have her hands in the workings of every board and pair of pants in New York City. It irritates me that she managed to convince Vince to drag me in for this, but honestly, as long as a vagina does the talking, it's not hard to convince Vince of feckin' anything. I should've expected it.

The shoot goes as well as I imagined it would—like sitting bare-arsed on an erupting volcano. Gloria makes a play for my cock, which I manage to block with a well-timed sidestep and an "accidental" flash of my camera that blinds the hell out of her. After I remind her I'm off limits to anyone but my future wife, she gives me an unaffected laugh and saunters out the door with a not-so-veiled warning to not keep her waiting much longer.

Now, as I stand in the middle of the makeshift photoshoot surrounded by a clumsily hung backdrop, shade umbrella, tripod, and light stands, I kick a wayward extension cord out of my way and curse the missed opportunity.

Where in the hell is Laken?

"Sorry, I'm late!" She rounds the corner, her wild blonde curls wet and plastered to her flushed cheeks. "It's raining outside, so I decided to catch a cab, and then there was this insane midtown traffic. I know you told me to be here at eleven, so when I looked at the time, I saw it was ten fifty-five, so I just bailed in the middle of Madison Avenue and ran the whole way here. You left my name at the front? Thanks for leaving my name at the front. I made a few wrong turns in this building, because fuck, this place is huge. Oh God, I didn't mean to say fuck! We're the only ones in here, right? I mean, there aren't any managers who could've possibly heard me say fuck to ruin my chances at—"

Crossing the few feet to where she stands, I place a hand over her mouth to stop her incessant talking. "Laken, breathe." She nods, the corners of her eyes pulling down in sheer panic. "There's no one here. It's just us. Take it down a few notches, aye?"

"Right," she agrees, brushing a piece of drenched hair out of her eyes. "So, what's the deal?"

"Deal?"

"Yeah, I mean, where's the fire? I bailed on my e-commerce class for this, Mackay. You said you had an amazing opportunity waiting for me at Trask and Payne." Taking off her rain jacket, she shakes it and splashes of water dampen my pants. "Am I meeting with company bigwigs? Did you get me the internship?"

Laken's eyes hold so much promise that a part of my stomach knots at the thought of dashing her hopes. I know I'm a shite for holding onto her as long as I can. As a single mother, she needs this job, but I know the minute I get her the internship she'll walk away. Am I a dick for dragging this out as long as I can? Maybe. Okay, probably, but in my defense, she *did* lose the bet at Turtle

Pond, so I'm under no obligation to cut our deal short.

"Not exactly," I answer honestly.

She stops mid-squeeze of her hair and gives me a pointed look. "Not exactly? What the hell does that even mean? What am I doing here, Niall?"

I wanted more of an audience for this, but beggars can't be choosers. I guess now is as good of a time as any. Dropping to one knee, I take her hand while reaching into my pocket. Laken's eyes widen, and her mouth rounds. I know this is supposed to be a pseudo-serious moment, but I can't help but think that this is the way I imagined her all those times in my shower. Only, I'd also imagined her down on her knees, her cheeks flushed just the way they are now as I slipped my cock between her—

"Niall, what the hell are you doing?"

Shite, had I actually closed my eyes? Oh feckin' hell, did I say something about her sucking my cock? If so, this will be over before it starts.

My eyes pop open, and before she can

slap me, I pull my hand out of my pocket. "Laken Cavanaugh, I knew ye were the one for me the minute my kid beat the shite out of ye kid at the park. Will ye marry me?"

I didn't think Laken's eyes could get any wider, but when I pull out my grandmother's two-point-five carat solitaire diamond ring, I tighten my hold on her hand, afraid she's going to pull one of those moves in those rom coms she's always talking about and pass out on me.

"Where did you get that?" she whispers.

"Family heirloom."

"You don't want to do this."

"I think I do."

I'm about to explain the virtues of public displays and office gossip when the mother of all office gossip proves my point before I can say a word.

"Holy shit! Niall, you Blarney-kissing motherfucker! Where have you been hiding her?"

As Laken gasps and turns around, I slip the ring on the third finger of her left hand before she can object. By the time she realizes what has happened, it's too late.

"Vince, meet my fiancée, Laken Cavanaugh." Even though Vince is in on my charade, Laken doesn't know that. So, in case she has any idea of blowing my cover, I add, "Laken, this is Vincent Tribiotti, project manager at Trask and Payne." Then I stand and lean in close to her ear. "In charge of screening intern applications."

He's *not* in charge of anything of the sort. I'm such a dick.

Laken swallows hard and pastes a plastic smile on her face, extending her newly minted hand. "It's a pleasure to meet you Mr. Tribiotti. Niall has told me so much about you."

Ever the arse, Vince gives her a wink and kisses the back of her hand. "Funny, Mackay has never mentioned you."

If looks could kill, the man would be six feet under. After Laken leaves, I plan on hitting him where it hurts. I know he has a thing for the brand-new promotions intern, and I plan on telling her exactly what kind of gobshite he really is.

Paybacks are a bitch.

However, Laken, covers like a pro. "Yes, well, our whole relationship happened very fast." She gives me a side-eye glare that makes me want to protect my dick from being separated from my body. "But any friend of Niall's is a friend of mine."

Vince slaps my arm and winks at her again. "Hold on to this one, Mackay. She's one of a kind."

You don't have to tell me.

"Don't ye have somewhere to be, Vince?"

"Right," he says, giving Laken one last full-length appraisal. "Just wanted to tell you that I passed the black widow on the way out. Whatever you said to her sent her horns up and her bitch radar on alert. If you aren't going to take my advice, I'd introduce her to Laken sooner rather than later."

"That's the plan," I say as I step forward and urge him out the door.

He holds my eye for a moment before reaching for Laken's newly-engaged finger and kissing her hand again. "A pleasure, Laken. I trust you'll save me a dance at the gala?"

Laken's eyes glaze over, but she answers automatically. "Of course."

Pushing him out of earshot, I leave Laken in the room as I walk him out of the conference room. "Kiss her again, and I'll cut ye lips off."

"Such violent threats over a fake fiancée, Mackay. What gives? Since this isn't real, can I have a crack at her when you're done? She's hot as fuck."

"Ye touch her, ye feckin' die." Giving him a harder shove than necessary, I slam the door.

Turning around to face Laken, I immediately hold up a hand to ward off her questions. "Look, I'm tired of the kid dates. The gala is tomorrow, and we've yet to spend any time alone. This shite stops tonight. If we're going to act like a couple, we need to be a couple. We're having drinks at the Scribe and Scholar tonight—just us. Alone. Ye got that?"

She stares at me for a moment, and I'm fully prepared for a Laken Cavanaugh argument. Instead, she cocks her head. "Fine. I have one question, though."

"What?"

"If things go south with this engagement, what happens?"

"What do ye mean?"

"Exactly what I said. If you don't get what you want, do I not get what I want?"

"I'm not following."

"Say someone finds out we're not really engaged and this whole thing is a sham. What happens to me? I didn't ask for this, Niall. You need to remember that. Whatever happens, you need to remember that *you* asked *me* for this."

"Don't worry, Laken," I snap, irritated at the turn of events. "I'll uphold my end of the bargain. Ye and Preston will be taken care of."

Her face blanches. "Right. Me and Preston."

That warning bell goes off again, but I can't figure out why. As I walk her out of the room, a nagging feeling follows me. It follows me all day and stays with me all night.

There's an old saying that goes, "When you love someone, you can't see the fault in that person."

Apparently, you can't see their lies either.

Chapter Seven

LAKEN

The Scribe and Scholar ends up being a low-key bar filled with dark furniture, dark lighting, and over twenty taps of beer. It's the kind of place where patrons go to unwind after a long day on Wall Street, which pretty much describes most of the clientele.

Men in pressed business suits crowd the round booths, slamming shots and nursing dark stout beers. They keep to themselves mostly, quietly chatting with friends, laughing over a joke here and there, and loosening their ties. The place is relatively small, and definitely not designed for the overly exuberant, drink till you puke crowd. I appreciate the darkness. If I run into anyone I know from NYU with this rock on my hand, I'm fucked.

Now ask me why I haven't taken it off since Niall slipped it on my finger.

Go ahead. I'm waiting.

Notice I haven't answered? The reason is because I have no fucking idea why.

The minute he put it on my finger, it was like the band fused with my skin. My mind knows everything is fake, but I'd be lying if I said I don't like the way it sparkles on my hand, or that I didn't write Mrs. Niall Mackay twenty-seven times with little hearts around it like I was back in eighth grade and crushing on the cute boy in class.

Keep rolling your eyes. Do you know the first rule of marketing? If you don't believe in what you're selling, the buyer will see right through you. That's Advertising 101, and it works in all facets of life. Don't believe me? Look it up.

Yep, eleven thousand dollars a semester to learn how to delude myself. I'm living the dream here, folks.

I'm sitting in a booth in the back alone, while Niall is outside calling to check on Sophie. I had a moment of panic when he asked if I needed to check on Preston as well, and I made up some shit about having just sent a text and that he was fine.

I'm going to hell for that one.

As I glance around the bar, my eye catches a patron at the bar who's nursing a highball and staring at me like I'm on the menu. Now, I'm not one of those holier-than-thou bitches. As you can see, I'm a prime example that those who live in glass houses cannot cast stones. However, one fake relationship per month is my limit, so deciding to use my newfound status to my advantage, I run my fingers across my face and make a huge production of flashing my ring. Diamonds are like kryptonite to some men, and I'm not shocked when he turns around in a huff.

Drumming my fingers on the table, I'm just about to check my watch again when the door opens, and Niall smiles as he makes his way over. Without hesitating, he slides in right beside me. Normally, I'd roll my eyes and make some comment about personal space. I mean, tell me I'm not the only one who sees couples do that same-side sitting shit in restaurants and wants to slap them? Unless your table is so huge that you need FedEx to deliver a salt shaker, scoot the fuck over, and eat like normal human beings.

But for some reason, the simple gesture from *him* flusters me in a way I'm not used to.

A moment of silence barely passes before a waitress in tiny shorts and a white crop top swings her hips over to our table and winks at Niall. "Hi, I'm Molly. What can I get you, handsome?"

I narrow my eyes at her and lift my left hand, tracing my bottom lip with the pads of my fingers.

Hi, bitch. I'm right here. See the ring?

Niall is oblivious to the whole thing, smiling like the village idiot at both of us.

Men.

Raising an eyebrow at me, he motions to the drink menu. "Laken?"

Molly can bring us two glasses of motor oil for all I care. I was over this the minute she walked over and opened her mouth. It's the jealous woman in me. We all have her inside us, and if a girl tells you any different, she's lying.

"Whatever you're having."

"We'll have two pints of Guinness and two shots of Irish whiskey." Niall holds up two fingers on each hand, because I suppose Molly's too stupid to comprehend the order without visual cues.

Molly winks again and leans over much farther than necessary to place cardboard coasters in front of him. Once she's sufficiently shoved her overinflated tits in Niall's face, she gives him a syrupy smile. "Be right back with that, sugar."

Wink at him again, and I'll fix that eye tick for you, honey.

Wait, why the hell am I being so territorial? Niall and I aren't a real couple. We're together for a purpose. That's it. There's no "us." So why does it make me so insane that this chick is hitting on him like there's a neon *available* sign flashing across his forehead? This is nuts. Nothing about today makes sense. My brain is twisting everything, making four and four somehow equal twenty.

Because there's no possible way that it can equal twenty, right?

After Molly disappears, I shake the fog from my head. "Beer and liquor? Be careful. A girl might think you're trying to get her drunk and take advantage of her."

Niall looks up, his gaze hooded and electric. "A girl might be right."

I can't help it, I burst out laughing. Not in the "ha-ha, what you said is asinine and ridiculous" way, but more in the "inappropriate giggle during a funeral" way.

I know, way to kill the moment, Laken. Just go right ahead and deflate the ego of the guy both you and Molly are lusting over. Well, cut me some slack. Nervous laughter is kind of my thing.

When I was a junior in high school, Bobby Herron and I were making out behind the gym after school. I was inexperienced, and he was a popular football player. Things got hot and heavy, but the minute he put my hand on his cock, I started laughing. I didn't mean to. I was just nervous. Yeah, the guy every girl wanted to be with and I laughed at his dick. Try coming back from that one. Guess how many dates I got after that?

"Come on, Laken. You're a college girl. Are you telling me you can't handle your liquor?" Niall's smile doesn't fade as he places his hand on my knee and squeezes.

Screw you, Bobby Herron.

I raise my chin in response to his challenge. "I don't drink much. When I'm not at school or studying, I'm with Preston."

Before I say anymore, Molly sashays her ass back over to the table with our drinks. I stare holes into her skimpy outfit and wonder what the maximum sentence is in New York for justifiable homicide when she brushes her hand with Niall's while handing him his drink. Just as I open my mouth to warn her she's going to pull back a nub if she touches him again, she hands me some fruity pink drink in a martini glass.

I frown. "I didn't order this."

Molly swivels around and points to one of the crowded barstools at the front of the bar. "I know. He did."

My eyes follow her pointed finger and land on the same guy from before. The one at the barstool who obviously has no regard for the sanctity of marriage.

Yes, I know. Hypocrite, party of one, your table is now available. That's like the toilet calling the outhouse full of shit. I get it.

Niall glances over his shoulder and lets out an aggravated groan. "Feckin' arsehole." Pressing his lips in a tight line, he furrows his brow and pushes the drink back toward Molly. "Send it back. She doesn't want it."

Something in my chest expands. Pride? Independence? An acute inability to shut my mouth?

"Excuse me?" I fire back. "I think I can answer for myself."

"Yes, and as your future husband, so can I. This bar is down the street from Trask and Payne, Laken. How will it look if ye accept drinks from other men while wearing my ring?"

I open my mouth to argue, but to my horror, no sound comes out. Damn him. I hate it when he's right. I hate it, even more, when he knows it.

Placing the drink on Molly's tray, he dismisses her and hands me my beer while raising his. "To the future Mrs. Mackay."

He chuckles as if we didn't just have some sort of minor standoff concerning our fake marriage and my fake rights as his fake wife. I sigh, wondering if achieving my dream this way is even worth it. "Cavanaugh-Mackay," I mumble as I take a small sip of the thick, dark beer, immediately coughing and spitting it out.

"Are ye all right?" he asks, trying and failing miserably not to laugh.

"This tastes like shit!" I blurt out. "What the hell kind of beer is this?"

It's wet and heavy and honestly tastes like a soggy scrap of molded bread. I don't want to be rude, but holy hell, I'd rather suck on battery acid.

Niall's eyes crinkle at the corners, his laughter finally getting the best of him. "It's Guinness, a nice pint of the black stuff. Official drink of Ireland."

"It's black, all right." I wrinkle my nose and push the offending glass away.

Still grinning, he takes a hefty drink from his own glass and smiles. "I thought all college girls were connoisseurs of this stuff."

"I told you, I'm a college girl, not a party girl. I have to keep my head on straight. One wrong move can affect a lot of people, not to mention my future."

He puts his glass down and gives me an inquisitive look. "Well, ye can't say shite like that and not follow it up."

"What is this, twenty questions?"

"Why, do ye have some deep, dark secrets ye are trying to hide?"

You have no idea.

I shrug and try to feign innocence. "What do you want to know?"

He studies me before speaking again. "Two truths, one lie."

Oh shit. I can feel my face fall, positive that I'm busted. "What?"

He motions to the whiskey. "Two truths, one lie. It's a drinking game my friends and I used to play all the time back in Dublin.

I'll give you three statements, and ye tell me which one is the lie. If ye guess correctly, I have to down a shot."

Okay, seems harmless enough. "That doesn't sound so bad."

He holds up a finger and smirks. "But if ye are wrong, ye have to slam one." Leaning in close, he brushes a stray hair off my cheek. "And just so ye know, I play to win, Laken. Ye should know this about me."

"Is that a threat?"

He winks and pushes my shot forward. "It's a warning. Now, I'm a gentleman, so I'll risk it first." Sitting back against the cushion of the booth, he pretends to think hard, the lines in his forehead deepening. "This is the first real date I've had in eight years, I love my job, and I absolutely fuck on the first date."

"Gentleman, huh? Is that why I'm the one with a drink in my hand instead of you?"

Niall wags a finger at me and takes another sip of his beer. "Ye are stalling."

"Well, while that's probably the most ballsy last statement I've ever heard, you're a guy, so it's probably true. That leaves me with the other two." I run my nail along the rim of the shot glass and squint an eye at him. "Let's see, you're good looking, outgoing, funny, and American women swoon over accents, plus you work for one of the most prestigious marketing firms in New York. I'm going with door number one. You've had lots of dates."

Like taking candy from a baby.

Never taking his eyes off me, he points to the shot of whiskey in my hand. "Drink."

"What? I got it wrong? No way."

"Do ye always take shite at face value, Laken? Somehow ye don't strike me as that gullible."

No way am I answering that. Lifting the shot off the table, I take a slow sip. "So, which one did I get wrong?"

"Are ye going to shoot that, or do I need to get ye a nipple for it?"

Nipple? Holy hell.

My head snaps up, and with one glance, my breathing becomes erratic and my thoughts go haywire. His penetrating stare is almost more than I can take, so I slam the shot, burn be damned and consequences be damned.

And apparently, the lining of my throat be damned, because fuck me, Irish whiskey is no joke. What the hell is in that shit? Liquid fire?

Niall watches me with curious eyes, ignoring my hacking coughs and gasps for breath. "I'm not a trusting person, Laken. I honestly don't see a need to date someone when I can get a good fuck or blow job for a hell of a lot less hassle."

"Well, that's straight and to the point."

"Ye aren't a fan of sex?" A vague smile plays at one corner of his mouth.

"Oh, I'm a fan," I admit, holding his stare. "I just think if you flirt with born-again virgin territory long enough, you start moving more toward fair-weather fan rather than die-hard."

"Now that's a shame," he says, raking a stare down the front of my dress. "Because one night with me, and I think ye position would change." Raising his gaze, the gold flecks in his eyes glitter. "Repeatedly."

Shit, did someone turn up the heat in this place? Suddenly I can't breathe. Focus, Laken! Hell, focus on anything other than the thought of him bending you over the—

"Tell me about your family," I blurt out.

Oh, well, that'll do it. Nothing limps a dick quicker than making a guy think about his mom.

But Niall just smiles. "They're still in Ireland. My Da owns his own pub. I grew up in that musty old place, but it was home. My Ma is a photographer too. She would take me out on her adventures, as she called them, to experience life. She always argued that I'd learn more in one afternoon of observing people through a lens with her than a week in school. She was right."

"She sounds like an amazing woman."

"She's the reason for my love of photography as well as my distrust of corporate America. Don't get me wrong, the Trasks and the Paynes are good people. I really like Nate and Rachel. I'm a pretty good judge of character, I think, but when you add in lawyers, middle management, accountants, shareholders, and board members, politics and greed tend to overshadow everything. People lie to get ahead."

People lie to get ahead.

People lie to get ahead.

People lie to get ahead.

The phrase repeats in my head like a broken record. A shudder tears through me, and I fight a wave of guilt. "Maybe they do it for reasons they wish they could explain."

Niall pins me with a hardened stare. "Have ye ever had ye life turned upside down because of lies and greed?"

"Well, no…"

"Sophie's mom came from money—a lot of money. Her parents wanted her to marry some rich, corporate guy like them, but instead, she found herself in my bed. We were careless kids and when she got pregnant, her parents gave her an ultimatum. Either she gave the baby up for adoption and walked away from me, or they disowned her. Jenna had a huge inheritance coming to her." He shrugs, his eyes blanking with a sadness that squeezes my heart. "Apparently, I wasn't worth risking it."

"She walked away? Just like that?"

"Just like that."

Alcohol gives me courage. "Then how did you end up with Sophie?"

He smiles wistfully. "Her parents are very prominent people. It didn't fit their public image to have their daughter step foot in an abortion clinic, so they hid her away until Sophie was born. I couldn't allow my child to go into the system, Laken. I knew I'd do it alone if I had to."

"She just handed over her own child?"

He nods. "I signed over all my rights to any money for me or Sophie in exchange for full custody. Jenna hasn't laid eyes on her since. It's hard making ends meet sometimes, but I wouldn't change a thing. That little girl is my feckin' world, and Sophie is better off without them."

"I can see that."

We sit in silence for a minute. As I twist my fingers in my lap, Niall reaches over and nudges me. "I'm sorry, I totally killed the vibe here. Let's get back on track. It's ye turn."

Somehow it seems in poor taste to go back to the game after that, but I humor him. "My favorite movie of all time is *My Best Friend's Wedding*, I've never been in love, and I've never gotten drunk in my life."

"I thought ye might make this hard on me," he jokes, cracking a smile again. "Definitely, the last one is the lie. Ye already told me ye are a rom com movie junkie, and I'm guessing with your piss-poor poker face during drinking games, ye been drunk at least once."

The warmth of the shot starts to work its magic as the room hazes. "Drink."

His eyebrows shoot up to his hairline. "Ye mean there's actually a rom com ye don't like?"

I stare at him, refusing to speak until he picks up the glass and tosses it back.

"Ye kidding me. Ye never been in love? What about Preston's father?"

I freeze. I don't mean for Preston's name to come up, and I have no idea how I'm going to get around this. Finally, I decide vagueness is my best bet at throwing him off. "Love is for idealists and dreamers. I barely knew him."

It's not a lie. Winston Hammerle is as elusive as Bigfoot. I'm not sure if he even exists, or if he's been created as a front so his wife can bulldoze her way into the right social circles.

Niall cocks his head to the side and studies me. "That's a little jaded, don't ye think?"

"Says the man who had to buy his own daughter."

"I'm sorry. I just can't believe a woman like ye has never had men fighting over her."

"No big deal. So, I've never been in love. It's not like I had great role models in that department. The only thing my mom ever loved were roadies and flashing her saggy boobs to aging rock stars."

"So, has Preston ever met his father?"

"A few times." I cross my fingers under the table and stretch the truth until it almost snaps. "But truthfully, his father is indifferent when it comes to him. Preston is a little eccentric and doesn't fit his mold of what an ideal son should be."

Niall's eyebrows lift. "He's wealthy too?"

Oh shit.

"You could say that."

He thinks for a minute, his fingers tightening around the glass. "Ye know, ye can sue him for child support. Don't accept this on ye own, Laken. That little boy deserve more. Ye both do."

Ugh. Preston does. I deserve everything coming to me.

"If ye want, I know some lawyers at Trask and Payne. I can make some calls for ye—"

"No!" I take a quick sip of the disgusting beer and shake my head while coughing and sputtering again. "I mean, that's okay. I do just fine on my own. I'm a private person, Niall. I'd prefer to keep it that way."

He regards me with a curious gaze, but his features relax and he seems to let the issue go. "So, what's so bad about *My Best*

Friend's Wedding to have made it on your cinematic shite list? Do ye have issues with weddings or are ye just anti-Julia Roberts?"

"You've never seen the movie, have you?"

"Can't say I have."

"It's a pseudo rom com." I stare down at my clenched hands, feeling as if I'm telling some sort of warped autobiography. "You know, the type that pulls the rug out from under you at the last minute. Those types are supposed to end all happy and make you believe in the stupid power of karma and love, right?"

"I suppose so."

"Well, there's this scene on a boat, the day before the guy Julia Roberts loves is supposed to marry someone else. It's the perfect setup for her to tell him not to do it because she loves him and you know he loves her. He even sings *The Way You Look Tonight* to her. How many clues does she need, for Christ's sake? If a guy sings that song to you, there's no way you can refuse."

"Good to know." Niall frowns. "Let me

guess, she doesn't tell him?"

"Fuck no," I blurt out with an impatient huff. "He even begs her—opens the door wide and tells her that if she loves him, to scream that shit out loud for once in her miserable life."

"Well, it's a rom com. Don't they end up together anyway?"

"No. That's why it's the shittiest rom com ever made. That douchebag marries the stick in the mud, and Julia Roberts loses everything." I slice a hand through the air. "Game over."

He drapes a hand across my thigh. "Well, considering ye have a ring on ye finger right now, things don't seem to be working out too badly for ye."

A smooth talker, my will to stay platonic, and my dignity walk into a bar...

There's no punchline here. All three walk in and only one is walking out. Any guesses on which one makes it home?

"Shots!" I call out to wherever the hell Molly disappeared to. "More shots!"

As if summoned by the word, Molly

suddenly appears—you guessed it—right by Niall's side with one hand on her hip and the other draped over his shoulder. If looks could kill, the bitch would be in a box with a concrete slab on top of her botoxed face.

She tosses a smile Niall's way. "How many?"

"Four," I answer before he does, and Molly looks like she just drank a pail of piss before swinging her overinflated ass back to the bar.

He blinks at me. "Four?"

I drum my fingers on the table, trying not to flinch at the thought of downing one, let alone two more of those vile drinks. "Scared?"

"Laken, I backpacked across Europe and lived in New York City with only a few dollars in my pocket." He chuckles and sits back, draping his arms across the back of the booth. "I don't know the meaning of the word."

Men are so easily distracted it isn't funny. Invading his personal space, I close the distance between us and press my lips against his ear, unable to hold back a smirk. "Well, Mr. Mackay, I suggest you put your drink where your mouth is and prove it."

Before I can pull away, he grabs ahold of my wrist and shifts so that our mouths are inches apart. "Play ye cards right, and I'll put it somewhere else."

This just got interesting.

"Do you always blatantly ask for sex?"

"Aye." His gaze drops to my lips, and I shudder. "Only from women whose middle name is Paige."

I'm so fucked.

When did I lose the upper hand, and why am I dying for him to just lean in and kiss me senseless? If I just brush forward, our lips will touch. Then the ball will be in his court.

No. This is not the time to lose focus and let sexual infatuation cloud my judgment. Niall Mackay holds my future in his hand, and I can't let some stupid attraction get in the way.

I pull away. "I think you're drunk."

"I think ye are changing the subject, Miss

Cavanaugh." Reaching for the shots Molly put on the table during our staredown, Niall places a shot glass in front of me and raises his own in the air while giving me a wolfish wink. "To what comes later."

Yeah. I'm definitely fucked.

Chapter Eight

LAKEN

Four shots become eight and by the time we stand to walk out of the bar, Niall acquires two more sets of eyes and has lips on either side of his face.

Or, I might be drunk and spinning. It's all new to me.

"You know?" I say as he places a hand at the small of my back. "You're not such... such a dick after all."

A chuckle trails from behind me. "You thought I was a dick?"

I nod, forgetting my head is no longer attached to my neck. It wobbles unsteadily until I hold onto a chair while attempting to stumble to the door. "Yep. I thought you were just as much of a bully as your kid. She knocked Preston down and wailed on him.

Did you teach her to fight like that or was her mom a WWE wrestler?"

A burst of warm air smacks me in the face as we walk outside. Niall still has his hand pressed against my lower back, guiding me away from the building, and my skin is tingling with the warmth of the whiskey. I can't help but feel a little guilty. The day has been amazing. The date has been amazing. Niall has been amazing.

And I'm an asshole. A shit. A lying shit. I should tell him the truth right now. Just get it all out and come clean. He'll probably call the whole deal off, which is what I deserve.

I almost do it.

Almost.

Until he runs a hand up my arm and pulls me to him. All I can smell is the forest. Hell, he smells like the forest. It's intoxicating, and all I want to do is curl up against him and breathe him in.

"Laken, I have to be honest with ye."

My head pops up from his chest at that word. "Honest?"

"Aye," he whispers, his Irish accent like

a drug. "I like the way things are headed with us. I want to ask ye…"

Ask me. Ask me. Ask me.

"Mackay! How the hell are you? I haven't seen you around the office since we finished the Brower account." I swallow hard as the same burly guy who'd sent me the drink earlier barrels out of the bar and claps Niall on the shoulder.

"Feckin' hell." Painting a forced smile on his face, Niall shifts away from the intoxicated man's hold and nods to him as he introduces me. "Laken, this is Bryce Holley, another project manager at Trask and Payne."

At the mention of Trask and Payne, I immediately perk up and try my best to act sober. Shit, why didn't I just accept the damn drink? If I'm going to be working with these people, I can't start off on the wrong foot.

Just as I extend my hand, Niall curses under his breath and gives me an apologetic look. "Damn. I left my credit card on the table. Laken, will ye excuse me for a moment?" Tossing a warning glare at Bryce, he nods toward the door. "I'll just be a minute."

As soon as the heavy wooden door closes behind Niall, Bryce licks his lips and steps toward me. "It's not polite to turn down a drink, Laken." His inebriated eyes trail down my dress with hunger. "Haven't seen you around. Are you new at the office?"

I don't like the wild look in this guy's eyes or the way he's undressing me with them. I step backward and end up flush against the brick wall of the bar. "No, I'm just a friend of Niall's."

"Any friend of Niall's is a friend of mine," he drawls, baring his stained teeth.

Ew. This guy amps the creepy vibe up to an eleven.

I turn my head away and push myself closer to the wall. "Yes, well, I have quite enough friends, thanks."

He braces his palms on either side of my head. "Come on, baby, don't play hard to get. You might regret it."

"Doubtful."

"Well, Niall is a friend of mine and we have an arrangement. What's mine is mine and what's his is mine." Pressing a knee between mine, he inhales long and hard against my neck.

Disgusted, I don't think, I just open my mouth and react. "Way to hit on your friend's fiancée. Go sleep it off, asshole."

"Is there something I can help ye with, Bryce?" There's a sharp edge to Niall's voice as he slams the heavy wooden door behind him. "Ye know, other than my fiancée?"

"Fiancée?" Bryce's bloodshot eyes waver briefly before the cocky smirk returns. "You might want to keep this one on a tighter leash, Mackay. She was on my dick the minute you walked away."

Niall lets out a low laugh that's not meant to be funny, and a chill runs down my spine. "Ye saw me walk in with her and sent the drink over anyway. I don't know what the hell ye are trying to prove, but touch her again, and I'll end ye, ye miserable feck." Niall takes a step forward, now almost chest to chest with Bryce, his eyes wild with untamed fury as he shoves him hard in the center of his chest.

Panicked that this is about to end up in some sort of pissing contest, I hold up one hand and pull on Niall's with the other. I should be irritated he doesn't think I can handle this on my own, but some deep-rooted part of me is turned on by his desire to protect me.

"It's not worth it," I whisper in his ear.

Bryce scrambles to his feet and spits on the ground in front of him. "This isn't over, Mackay." Giving me one last glare, he disappears around the corner.

We stand there in silence until Niall turns and touches my cheek with fire in his eyes. "Did he touch ye?"

"It's fine, I—"

His jaw tightens with every word. "Did. He. Touch. Ye?"

"No," I admit, the sexual electricity between us almost too much to take. His stare is heated, and if I hold it too long, I'll get lost in it forever. "Well, thanks for tonight, Niall, I—"

An impending storm of rage flashes through his eyes as he roughly grabs my

147

cheek and claims my mouth in a heated kiss. I've wanted him to kiss me again for so long, but for some reason, the guilt of everything is eating at me. I push the nagging remorse down and for half a heartbeat, we stand there, tongues clashing and fingers tugging at each other's hair before I finally come to my senses and pull away.

"I need to...this is...I need to go home, Niall."

A half smile plays on his lips as he caresses my cheek, leaving one last lingering kiss on the corner of my mouth. "I'll walk ye."

The whole way back to my apartment, the sexual chemistry is blinding. Niall is affectionate and attentive, and I battle back and forth between giving in and ending the lie right now.

The minute we reach the door to my apartment, Niall braces a hand on each side of the doorframe and boxes me in. "Sophie is at a sleepover with a neighbor tonight."

I smile and eye him curiously. "Are you flirting with me, Mackay?"

His face flushes, but I know the minute his eyes darken, it's not embarrassment staining the skin above his beard. "No, I was flirting with ye back at the bar. Now, I'm propositioning ye."

He looks so sure of himself that it unnerves me. "Well, that's blunt."

His voice rumbles as he crowds me against the door. "Aye. When there's something right in front of me I know I want, I see no reason to mince words." Taking a step closer, he presses his body against me, and every nerve ending blazes with electricity. "What do ye want, Laken?"

There's a right answer and a wrong answer here. One that's responsible and one that serves my own selfish, horny needs. "You," I whisper on a breathy exhale.

With my back pressed up against my door, Niall smiles a devilish grin that causes that adorable dimple to sink deep into his cheek, and I can almost believe our lie is real—that there's emotion behind the heat in his eyes, and he feels something for me. I bite my lip, realizing I'm in over my head. The line between fake fiancée and reality has blurred so much that I can't see this for what it really is—just simple drunken lust.

Then he kisses me again, and I lose all concept of right and wrong. I can't think. I can barely breathe. Niall Mackay's kisses are as hypnotic as his accent, and combined, they flip my world inside out and upside down. The roughness of his assault and the way he commands control of my lips drown me. I'm quickly losing every reservation I have against inviting him inside.

Finally breaking the kiss, Niall pulls back and cups my cheek. "Is Preston coming home tonight?"

Who?

Preston. Preston. Preston. Oh fuck! Panic squeezes my heart, so I say the first thing that comes to my mind. "Preston is spending the night at a friend's house too."

Technically it's not a lie. Technically, Lollie is a friend, and technically, she lives at the Hammerle estate where technically, Preston lives as well.

Also? Technically, I'm full of shit.

"I'm not an exhibitionist, Laken, but if ye don't open the door, ye neighbors are going to get to know a whole new side of ye." Although he laughs, there's a darkness in his stare that has my palms pressing flat against the wood and my fingers twitching with restraint.

And this is where I break my neck trying to open the door.

Digging blindly in my purse for my keys, I close my hand around the bundle of metal clanging together. Finally finding the right key, I jab it into the lock a few times before it finally fits, and I sigh with relief when it turns. I can hear Niall breathing heavily behind me, and the only thing on my mind is what he's going to sound like on top of me. Even the thought has my palms sweating as I hurry to push the door open.

Then it hits me.

I'm supposed to be a single mom. There's supposed to be a kid living here with toys and shit a six-year-old boy would like. Not the last six issues of *Vogue* and the complete box set collection of *Sex And The City* on DVD.

"I don't think—"

"That's the problem," Niall growls, his accent growing heavy with desire. "Ye think too much. Way too feckin' much." Before I can object, he snakes a hand around me and turns the doorknob.

The minute I fall backward into my apartment, I lose my hold on all reservations as well as my sanity. I'm doing this. I am *so* doing this. Screw morals, screw what's right. Go ahead and call me every name in the book for my deception, or bending of the truth, or whatever the hell you want to label it. Tonight, I'm going to be immoral as fuck. I'll worry about the consequences tomorrow.

Holding a finger against his lips, I shake my head and take a deep breath. "One second."

"What the hell for?"

My anxiety heightens as out of the corner of my eye, I see Shelby's bedroom door standing wide open. Anatomy diagram posters and framed certificates and awards hang on the walls like a shining beacon to my lies. My gait falters as more broken lies tumble from my mouth.

"Didn't clean. Shit everywhere. Be right back." Running toward Shelby's door, I lock it from the inside, slam it closed, and give it a quick tug to ensure no one can get inside. I know Shelby has a shift at the hospital until six a.m., so there's no chance of her showing up and shitting all over my parade.

I barely turn around when Niall fists my hair and gives it a firm tug backward. His lips are on me before I can react, and my mind blanks. It's frantic. It's hot. It's about to happen right here against Shelby's door if we don't move.

"Bedroom," I mumble against his lips.

As soon as we stumble through the door into my room, Niall kicks it closed, and our hands and mouths are everywhere. One minute I'm facing the door, and half a heartbeat later, he's spinning me around and slamming me so hard against it all the air rushes out of my lungs. Entwining our fingers, he lifts my arms over my head and pins them against the wood. He's holding me immobile, and I pause, expecting his dominance to trigger my fight or flight instinct to rear its ugly head. Instead, all it does is amp up my already explosive desire, and I press myself harder against his rigid body.

"Christ, Laken," he mumbles against my lips. "I'm feckin' tasting every inch of ye tonight." Reaching behind him with one hand, he pulls his T-shirt over his head and tosses it aside.

I swallow hard as I roam my eyes down his body. His chest is hard and defined. It's beautiful, and I want it pressed against me in the worst way. Not waiting for a response, he dives his tongue deep between my lips again, tangling mercilessly with mine as we both fight for air.

I have no idea what I'm doing.

That's a lie. I know exactly what I'm doing, and I have no intention of stopping. What I don't know is why that little voice inside me that normally stops me from being impulsive and irrational isn't screaming at me in her usual shrill voice to start thinking with my head instead of my hormones.

I'm not used to casual sex. Hell, I'm not used to sex period. If I got laid on a regular basis, maybe I wouldn't be pushed up against my bedroom door like a starving dog in heat and could think clearly.

Niall wraps his hands around my face and stares at me. My stomach flips, and I feel a level of exposure I'm not sure I'm comfortable with, so I lower my gaze to the floor. He stops me, his grip on my cheeks tightening as he lifts my chin.

"What's holding ye back, Laken?"

"I don't know. Before, it was…it was all pretend. Here, with you and me like this? This is real. You're real. What we're doing is real. We can't uncross this line once it's crossed."

There it is. What's been bothering me since we left the bar. Once we have sex with this lie between us, the game changes. It will no longer be as simple as handing the ring back to him and walking away at the end of the night.

What happens when the clock strikes twelve? Is Cinderella left with only one shoe and memories of one really amazing night, or does she get the prince, the mice, the job, and the corner office?

Spreading his thumbs across my cheekbones, Niall runs his nose from my ear down the slope of my neck, his hot breath igniting an inferno that has been building all night. Placing a light kiss at the base of my throat, he brings my face against his until our noses touch. "I want to cross every line with ye, Laken. It's time to drop all the bullshite. Just us and a question."

"I've already said I'd fake marry you. What other question could you have?"

Niall lowers his hold and stares at me, his jaw twitching and heat glinting in his amber eyes. "Well, if we're going to have a fake engagement, then I figure we should be able to bypass the fake marriage and get to the fake honeymoon."

"I still don't hear a question in there."

"My mistake. Let's make this official." Tugging my hips hard against him, he grinds his thick erection into me while whispering against my lips. "Do ye, Laken Cavanaugh, want me to have ye right here? To drive my cock so deep into ye that ye feel me for days afterward? To take ye right here against this door so hard ye won't be able to walk through one again without screaming my name?"

Oh, hell yes, please. All that and more.

I whimper as he shoves a knee between my legs and pins me harder against the door. "I'm sorry, Miss Cavanaugh. Could ye speak up? Ye seem to have lost that smart arse mouth."

"Yeah. I mean, I do. I will. Mmmhmm."

And that is the exact opposite of how to talk dirty to your man. I promise you, in my head, all sorts of naughty phrases like, "give it to me," or "my pussy aches for you," roll through my mind. But me being me, what comes out instead? Yeah and Mmmhmm.

"Well," he says, grabbing the back of my thigh and hitching my leg around his waist. "By the power vested in me by the fact that I'm two seconds away from ripping off that tiny scrap of lace ye call panties, I now pronounce us about to fuck like wild animals. Ye may now kiss the man who's about to make ye come harder than ye came in ye life."

"I, uh—" I swallow the rest as Niall crushes his lips to mine.

Men, if you want to shut a woman up, there's a right way and a wrong way to do it. Telling her to shut up? Wrong way. Absolutely the wrong way, and nine times out of ten, you should probably sleep with your hand over your dick. Quieting her with a passionate kiss that curls her toes and makes her forget her own name? That's going to end happily for both of you. Trust me on this.

Alcohol swims through my veins and as his one hand holds my thigh tight on his hip, his other snakes under my dress. I gasp as he runs a finger down my panties, circling the damp fabric.

I know I said it has technically been

a while since I've had sex, but it's not like you forget the mechanics of how it's done. You especially don't forget how the tease of a hand can send your mind racing over to the other side of crazy. And that's how Niall Mackay makes me feel. Certifiably crazy. Like losing my hold on reality and skydiving without a parachute.

Niall groans my name as his kisses grow harder and more forceful. I have no idea what's come over me to egg him on like this, but he's pushed me past the point of thinking this through. All I can think of is having the cock that's pulsing against my stomach lodged deep inside me.

As he grazes his teeth down my throat, I somehow manage to find my voice. "Don't make promises you can't keep."

His eyes widen as he lifts his head, and a wicked smirk curves his lips. He doesn't answer me, only slips his finger underneath the edge of my panties and presses it lightly over my clit. Sparks shoot across my field of vision, and I ache for more. Groaning, I push against him, wanting him to touch me more than I've wanted anything in a long time. With a chuckle, he makes a light pass over my clit again, circling it with the tip of his finger, and before I have a chance to protest, he slides it down my wetness and drives it inside.

Holy. Fucking. Shit.

As he finds his rhythm, he adds a second finger and returns attention to my throbbing clit with his thumb. I'm now clawing the door and riding his hand as pure heat incinerates me from the inside out. The minute he leans down and sucks my breast through the thin fabric of my dress, incoherent babble falls from my mouth, and honestly, I'm not even sure I'm speaking English as the voodoo he's working causes a thunderous orgasm to buckle my knees and shatter my world. Crying out his name, I slump against him and bury my forehead into his chest.

"Jesus!" I pant.

Releasing my leg, Niall hooks a finger underneath my chin and forces my eyes on his. Once he's satisfied I'm focused on his hooded gaze, he takes his finger and suck it deep into his mouth, swirling his tongue around it, approval rumbling deep in his throat.

"Feckin' delicious. Just like I thought."

Something dark shifts in his eyes, and my lips part. Not sure how much more I can take, I plead with him. "Niall…"

Removing his finger from his mouth, he traces it across my own lips as he fists my hair with his other hand. Involuntarily my tongue darts out before my lips close around his finger. If he weren't holding me, I'd probably drop to the floor.

Stepping back, he reaches in his pocket and pulls out a foil packet and holds it up between us. "You do it."

"Um, what?"

"Touch me, Laken. I want your hands on me."

He doesn't have to ask me twice. I'm primed and ready for him. Reaching between us, I unhook his belt, shocked to see my hands are steady and not at all shaking. Emboldened by my own assuredness, I make quick work of his zipper and push down his jeans, gasping as my hand touches his hot length.

He's huge. I don't mean, "Oh, wow, that's going to feel nice," huge. I mean, "Holy fuck, the man should bronze it and hang a picture frame around it," huge.

I must be staring because an impatient groan tears from his throat. "Laken…" Quickly rolling the condom on, I barely have time to look up before he slams my back against the door and, reaching under my dress again, rips the flimsy string holding my panties together. "Wrap your legs around my waist," he commands hotly in my ear.

Readily obeying, I hook my legs around him, and his fingers dig into the flesh of my ass. Rearing back, he gives a sharp thrust upward. A tiny squeak slips out, and that's all I manage before he pulls out and drives back in, repeating the move over and over until I'm about to lose my mind. Our combined groans along with the sound of skin slapping are the only things I hear beyond the unforgiving wood slamming against my spine.

Niall fucks like a man possessed, alternating punishing thrusts with smooth, long plunges. Sweat drips down my brow, and I feel my muscles clench around him.

"Niall! I'm coming again!"

"Do it. Come, baby," he growls in his deep Irish accent, his teeth sinking hard into my shoulder.

Screaming, I stiffen as my orgasm rips through me with a relentless intensity that rocks me until I don't even know my own name and the only one on my tongue is his. Niall powers inside me, spurring aftershocks that cause another round of spasms.

"Christ!" He lets out a tortured groan into the hollow of my neck and jerks inside me, bottoming out as his thrusts slow and eventually still.

Coming down from the high, I suddenly feel awkward. What we just did complicated an already bizarre situation. How can we walk away from each other now? How the hell will it be possible to stage a public breakup and still work together after this?

Millions of questions float through my

head as Niall shifts our bodies, still buried deep inside me, and heads toward my bed.

"Where are we going?" I ask, confused as to why he's not getting dressed and leaving.

He chuckles as he lowers us both to the bed and climbs over me. "If you think the honeymoon's over, Mrs. Mackay, you need to brush up on your rom coms."

"But…"

That's the last word I speak as Niall begins a heated trail of kisses down my stomach, and the minute he finds his destination, my world explodes for the third time.

Chapter Nine

NIALL

The ruse is over.

It stopped the minute she scraped her nails down my back and screamed my name. The sun is barely peeking through the blinds in her apartment as her bare arse presses up against me. We're entwined, spooned together, her back to my front, completely naked in her bed, and for the first time in my life, I'm not panicking. I don't have the insatiable urge to disappear before she wakes up or leave cab fare on the dresser while I spend the morning drinking coffee at Starbucks until she gets the hint that I'm not coming back.

It scares me how right this feels. When I said the vows to Laken last night, part of me meant them. Some deep and crazy mental part of me wanted to pretend they were real. That maybe I'd wake up this morning and they wouldn't have been just words said during amazing sex.

She's asleep, but I hope to feckin' hell last night meant something to her. I can't recall the number of women I've fucked in my life, but never have I lost myself in one like I did Laken Cavanaugh. I watched her. I drowned in her. I wanted to bury myself inside her and never leave. After fucking her against the door, I carried her to her bed and spent the entire night loving her body with my cock, my tongue, my fingers… hell, anything I could touch her with. As I whispered what I wanted to do to her in her ear, I willed her to read between the lines to hear what wasn't in my voice but what was in my heart. To see that this wasn't just a one-night stand for me.

"I want to taste you all night."

I want you forever.

"You're so wet for me."

You're the one I've waited for all my life.

"I want you so much."

I think I might love you.

I hope she felt it in the way I made love to her that I don't want her for just one night. I want her and Preston forever.

We fucked all night and early into the morning. Even when she fell asleep, I stayed awake and watched her sleep, knowing I'd dipped a toe into unknown waters I had no idea how to navigate my way through.

And now, in the early morning, I know screwed doesn't begin to cover what I am. Unable to take the rejection I know is coming, I give her one last kiss behind her ear and slip out of bed before she can give me the speech I dread hearing.

As I close the front door to her apartment, for the first time since uttering the phrase to Gloria that started this whole mess in the conference room of Trask and Payne, I wonder if I can pull this off tonight, or when it's all over, I'll lose my job, Sophie's future, and most importantly, the woman I don't think I can live without.

I've heard the phrase "take my breath away," but I've never experienced it until I arrive outside Laken's apartment dressed in my tuxedo and stand anxiously waiting for her to open the door. The minute I see her wearing what can only be described as floor-length satin sin, the phrase makes more sense than anything ever has in my life. She still looks beautiful, but there's an edge to her tonight that borders on seductress.

The dress seems modest in the front, with a thick tie that wraps around her neck and dips low enough in the front to show off her ample assets, but not scandalous enough to seem suggestive. It melts into a body-hugging turquoise satin number that pools at her feet with a thigh-high split that allows a hint of her leg to peek through when she walks. However, that's where the demureness ends. The minute she turns around, I have no doubt that dicks everywhere will salute her, thanking God that she walks the Earth. The entire back of the dress is bare, the base of the material resting at the top of her arse and barely hugging the sides of her breasts. The skin of her shoulders and back are coated in some sort of shimmery glitter that catches the light when she moves, holding my eyes hostage. She's all I see. She's all I breathe. The world around her ceases to exist. I've never seen anything so exquisitely beautiful in my life.

Breathtaking.

But what does it for me are the shoes. My eyes are held prisoner by crystal-encrusted stiletto fuck-me heels that elevate her legs in a way that forces my mind on nothing but having them draped over my shoulders at the end of the night.

"Eyes up here," she laughs with a throaty chuckle, bringing my attention back to her face.

Ladies need to learn one thing. It's all about the heels. High heels and nothing else will have a man on his knees begging for mercy. Forget the expensive lingerie.

"Shoes stay on," I barely manage on a whisper.

Bending one knee, she seductively

braces her heel against the wall. "Well," she says, hooking a finger under my chin and bringing my attention to her heavily smoky eyes. "It'd be rude to take them off at the party, now wouldn't it?"

"No, I mean after the party. Keep the shoes on when I fuck ye."

Bringing her lips within a breath of mine, a wicked smile plays on Laken's mouth as she licks her wine-stained lips. "Let's just see how tonight goes, shall we, Mackay? Depending on how well things go, I just may fuck *you*."

Funny how foreshadowing works, huh?

In my head, I hear, "If we pull off this charade and both get what we want, I'll ride ye until we can't walk tomorrow."

I have no clue that Laken's words are literal.

More than once, I consider asking the cab driver to make a detour and drop us off at my apartment instead of the gala. Even as we pull up outside the hotel, with swarms of paparazzi and reporters crowding the entrance, the thought still crosses my mind, especially when she grabs my hand and gives it a squeeze, my grandmother's ring sparkling brilliantly on her finger.

Once inside, we mingle a bit before making our way to the bar. "I'm so nervous." Laken smooths the front of her dress for the hundredth time and accepts her martini from the bartender.

Within three sips, half of the liquid is gone and I can't help but smile to myself. The last time she drank, she let her guard down, and I spent the night buried so deep inside her I thought I'd never find my way out. I'm hoping for a repeat performance.

"You'll be fine," I remind her, slipping my hand into hers. "Don't let them intimidate ye. Just stick to the facts we've talked about and if ye are unsure about anything, get them talking about themselves. These arseholes love nothing more than to talk about how great they are."

"How are you so calm? We're lying

to your bosses, and both our asses are on the line. Getting everything we want is contingent on how well we can sell this."

How can I be so calm? *Calm*? I'm not feckin' calm. I'm anything but calm. I'm a mess inside. My stomach is churning, my head is pounding, and my heart—well, hell. Let's not even talk about what a bleedin' hole that thing has become. All I know is that it aches because I'm about to introduce the woman on my arm as my fiancée, and as much as we've planned for this, I don't want it to be for just one night. I don't want her to take off that ring when this is over and hand it back to me.

I want more.

Squeezing her hand, I steer her away from the main ballroom and toward a darkened hallway. "We need to talk…"

Before we can turn the corner, salt and pepper gelled hair fills my line of sight, and Mr. Navarro stops me with a friendly hand on my chest. "And who is this beauty, Mackay? I half expected to see little Sophie with you tonight." A nod to Laken clarifies his statement. "You know, seeing as how this is a charity benefit for your daughter's school."

Lacing my fingers with hers, I pull Laken toward me, some deep-rooted caveman vibe taking over my normal, outgoing demeanor. "Laken Cavanaugh, meet the marketing director at Trask and Payne, Gerald Navarro. Gerald, I'd like ye to meet Laken Cavanaugh," I pause as I speak the words I've waited twenty-eight days to say. "My fiancée."

I steal a quick glance at Laken, whose face is frozen in a forced smile. She's waiting, as am I, for his response. After a few moments of silence, Navarro's lips twitch, as a smile builds at the corners until they turn up into a full-hearted laugh. Throwing his head back, he slaps me on the back of the shoulder and beams. "It's about damn time, Mackay! And I don't blame you for keeping this one under wraps." Lowering his voice, he leans in and winks at Laken. "Better to solidify things before subjecting her to the likes of Tribiotti."

After walking the red carpet, taking

173

the obligatory pictures, and listening to Trask and Payne bigwigs make their inflated speeches, I've introduced Laken to Mr. Navarro and all the people who'd be responsible for hiring her as an intern and an eventual hire. Everything is falling into place, but unfortunately, I have to leave her alone with Vince for a while to actually do my job and take the official pictures of the event. It takes me twice as long to do what I need to do because after every shot, I'm scanning the dance floor and shooting death glares at my friend.

Click.

Vince holding her close.

Click.

Vince looking into her eyes and flashing her a smug smile.

Click.

Vince twirling her around the dance floor, forcing a giggle out of her that makes me want to throat punch him.

Even though I'm the one who put Laken in his arms, it irritates the hell out of me to watch him dance with her. He's holding her much too close, and she's laughing way too loudly at his stupid jokes. I asked him to keep an eye on her while I worked, but even though he's my friend, I don't trust him. The minute he lowers a hand to the base of her spine and dips her low, my hand curls around my camera, almost snapping it in two with jealousy.

Agitated, I force myself to turn my away. That's it. I'm done. After tonight, I'm telling Laken that all bets are off. I'm done pretending. I'll live up to my side of our bargain and do everything in my power to get her job at Trask and Payne, but I'm not giving her up. There's something between us. I feel it, and I'm not letting it go.

Scanning the dance floor, I lock eyes with Laken. She gives me a small smile and dangles her fingers over Vince's shoulder in an unintentionally sexy wave. I lose my breath. I feckin' lose my breath, and my dick jumps to attention just from a smile.

There are countless women in this room who could buy and sell her twenty times over. Women who wipe their arses with hundred dollar bills and spend their lives in the limelight, networking with New York's finest. However, none of them can hold a candle to Laken Cavanaugh. She's the star of the show, and I'm the envy of every man in the room.

That's how I know this shite has to end now.

Just as I move to cut in on their dance, a hand snakes across my back. "I hope you saved me a dance."

I grit my teeth and purposely keep my back toward her. "I'm working, Gloria."

She seems slightly amused at finding me alone. "Where's your fiancée? I ran into Bryce Holley and he told me I should make sure I introduced myself tonight."

Fecker.

"She's busy."

Gloria continues as if I didn't speak, trailing her nails down the length of my spine. "I knew you'd show up alone, Niall. You've been avoiding me for weeks, but it stops tonight. My generosity is over."

I fix my eyes on Laken through the lens

of my camera, but I can almost feel Gloria's stare on me as she slips a key into my pocket.

"I'm tired of being made to wait." Patting my pocket, she leans in close. "Room five-sixteen. You either show up and give me what I want, or you can find a new job and Sophie can find herself a new school."

The band finishes playing their song and the room quiets. I've never raised my hand to a woman, but I've never wanted to hit one so much in my life as I do right now. If Gloria had a dick swinging between her thighs, she'd already be on the ground with my fist between her eyes.

However, even as our voices rise and eyes turn our way, I rein in my control and turn to face her, dismantling the lens on my camera with more force than necessary. "Threats again?"

Standing in a floor-length, bright red strapless gown, Gloria has her hair swept up in a similar style to Laken's. But whereas Laken's looks effortlessly classy and feminine, Gloria's tightly pulled twist is as harsh as the daggers flying out of her eyes.

"Facts, Niall. And were it not for the fact that my son is here, I'd make a scene right now and bury you." Gathering her composure, she pats her overly-sprayed hair and nods to the camera still gripped in my hand as she tosses back a glass of champagne. "Now take our picture so I can send him home with my maid, since my so-called nanny had better things to do tonight than her job."

"Ye son?" The words rub me the wrong way. That same unsettled feeling I've had all night twists my insides again.

She lets out a small sigh as she snags yet another glass of champagne off a passing hostess tray. "Yes, my son goes to Ravenhill too, Niall. You *do* remember that this is a benefit for them, don't you? I need pictures of me being the doting mother."

"Wait, he's here? Tonight?"

"Nothing gets by you, does it?"

Walking in, I'd made the decision to protect Laken from Gloria. But this bitch pushes all my buttons and has now forced my hand. If she wants to see a doting mother,

I'll show her a real one.

"Come with me," I say, grabbing her elbow and pulling her toward the dance floor.

"Thanks," she smirks, "but I'm not in the mood to tango."

"And I'm not in the mood for ye to carry on with ye feckin' bullshite," I warn with a growl, making my way toward Laken and Vince. I'm putting all of this to rest. Everything ends tonight. I'll get Gloria off my back, Sophie will be safe, my job will be safe, and somehow, I'll convince Laken we're meant to be together.

I'm feeling confident about my decision until I catch Laken's eye. The moment she sees me, she stumbles out of Vince's hold, her eyes wide with terror. Everything seems to happen in slow motion as she glances between Gloria and me, backing away and tripping over the back of her long gown.

Then things go from bad to worse as Bryce Holley appears by Gloria's side and opens his mouth. "Gloria, have you met Mackay's new fiancée?"

Gloria laughs hysterically. "Laken Cavanaugh? What the hell are you doing here?"

Laken gasps. "Lady Hammerle?"

I suck in a harsh breath at the sound of Laken's name on Gloria's lips. "Ye know each other?"

"Niall, man, are you all right?" Vince breaks in, lifting an eyebrow. "You're pale as shit."

All right?

All *feckin'* right?

Nothing about what's happening is all right. The woman I lied to, who wants to fuck me, and the woman I lied with, who I'm currently fucking, already know each other. In what universe is this okay? In what scenario does this not equal disaster?

Laken covers her mouth with both hands, shaking her head repeatedly as if doing so will teleport her out of the ballroom. "Holy shit, *you're* the black widow?"

Gloria's pupils dilate as she turns and glares at me. "You called me a black widow?"

I shake my head. "Not important, Gloria!

Can we please focus on how ye know each other?"

"Laken!" Out of nowhere, Preston, who's dressed in the smallest tuxedo I've ever seen, runs across the dance floor and hurls himself into Laken's arms. Stunned, Laken catches him and gives him a stiff embrace.

"Hi, Pres."

Bracing myself for the answer I don't want to hear, I ruffle Preston's blond hair while keeping my eyes on Laken. "Hey there, Preston. Don't ye mean Mommy?"

If possible, Laken's face pales even more, and tiny beads of sweat break out across her forehead. "Niall, I can explain."

Realizing what's about to happen, I ask the words anyway. "Laken, why is ye son here?"

"Her son?" Gloria straightens, reining in the shock that somehow managed to register on her expressionless face. "Preston is *my* son."

"No, he's Laken's son."

Gloria narrows her eyes, and as realization blankets her face, a guttural laugh rumbles deep in her throat. "Oh, this is almost worth everything." She shifts a finger between Laken and me. "So, you concocted this story to make me think you were engaged, and you were the one who ended up getting played."

I can't hear a word she's saying. All I can concentrate on are the tears running down Laken's face as she hugs Preston to her chest.

"Oh, get over yourself, Niall," Gloria continues. "Laken has been my nanny for over a year and a half. I had a planned C-section at thirty-six weeks with that boy." A smug smile paints her lips as she leans in close. "I have no stretch marks because of it. Do you want to see?"

"Laken?" Preston asks, tugging on one of Laken's curls that has escaped from her pinned hairstyle. "Is Sophie here? Mommy, I've had so much fun with Laken and Sophie and Niall."

With a devious gleam in her eye, Gloria claps her hands and raises her voice. "Well, isn't this special? Everyone, can I have your attention, please? My son's nanny is engaged to our own Niall Mackay." Cuing the band to return to the stage, she grabs as many champagne flutes from a passing tray as she can hold. "Maestros? Can we hear a little *Here Comes the Bride*? This has turned into an engagement party!"

Gloria hands me a champagne flute, and I freeze as she walks by Laken, who's clinging to Preston like a life preserver. Taking a long sip, she leans in close and whispers so low, I barely hear her voice. But there's no mistaking the words I read on her lips.

"Oh, and by the way, you're fired. Get your shit and get out."

And just like that, my world ends.

Chapter Ten

LAKEN

Present Day

Back to Jack from *Titanic*.

Even when he knows the ship is going down, and he'll most likely end up as shark bait, he keeps his game face on. Regardless of how many icicles hang from his perfect blond hair or how blue his lips get, the guy has this never say die attitude.

You have to respect that. The chips are down, the band is playing a medley of songs to die by, and people are dropping like flies off the side of the boat right into the frigid water, but that son of a bitch never gives up.

So why in the hell am I sitting on my couch at six a.m. in an evening gown, stuffing my face full of ice cream, half drunk, and feeling sorry for myself when I should be climbing to the top of my own sinking ship instead of going down with it?

Good question. Maybe because I'm a glutton for punishment. Or a moron. Or hopelessly in love. Can you be in love after only four weeks?

Never mind. I'll answer my own question. Yes, you can, because I'm head over heels in love with Niall Mackay. I just didn't know it until I lost him. Now, after making myself sick off ice cream and cheap wine, I know there's only one thing left to do.

Tossing the demolished ice cream carton on the coffee table, I chuck the spoon across the room and discard the empty wine bottle on the floor. The ship may be sinking, but it hasn't gone completely under yet.

I'm going to do what I should've done six hours ago. I just hope it's not too late.

Grabbing my phone, I call for reinforcements. When she picks up, I don't even bother with pleasantries. "Do you still have those security tapes we saved on that flash drive for a rainy day?"

"Of course," Lollie clips, as if offended I'd have to ask. "Why?"

"Email them to me."

"Why?" she repeats, a slight edge in her tone.

"Because there's about to be a fucking tsunami."

Threatening Gloria Hammerle ended up being the highlight of my year. No, I take that back. Watching her cave under pressure and dissolve into a bucket of tears at my feet was the highlight of my year. Threatening her just felt fucking fantastic.

After spending the better part of a decade as the Hammerle housekeeper, Lollie had made friends with the gardener, the chef, the maintenance workers, and most importantly, the head of security. Not surprisingly, they all loathed Gloria as much as we did and took great pleasure in passing along security tapes of every sordid sexual escapade she had on the grounds. Lollie kept them all on a backup file, calling them her little insurance policy for a rainy day.

As I ran out of the Trash and Payne gala without an explanation or a goodbye to anyone, I heard Gloria threaten to have Niall fired and Sophie thrown out of Ravenhill. The floods were rising, and I had to act quickly. Convincing Lollie to be my partner in crime wasn't hard. She'd been waiting for a moment like this and gleefully emailed me every pornographic detail that was now burned into my retinas for all of eternity.

With the blackmail in my hand, it was almost poetic to have Gloria meet me at the same park where I'd first met Niall. The perfect place for justice to be served.

Once I showed her the footage, she folded like a cheap house of cards. Gone was the bravado of Lady Hammerle, her nose stuck so high in the air she could trip over a pebble and break her neck. All that was left of her sat on a bench in Central Park in a velour track suit with mascara running down her face, begging me not to send the file to her husband.

Apparently, there was a prenup involved, and that prenup included a cheating clause.

Do you see the shit-eating grin on my face? Just wait, it gets better.

With a written agreement—because I'm not a moron—Gloria agreed to leave Niall and Sophie alone and to step down from the board of directors of Trask and Payne. I also made sure she gave me visitation rights with Preston.

Didn't think I had that kind of power, did you? Me either.

Apparently, when someone's bare ass is on the line—and the pool table, and the chaise lounge, and the kitchen island—a shift of power can happen in the grunt of an orgasm.

See what I did there?

Now, half an hour after Gloria ran off in a sniveling tirade of tears, I'm still here. I'm still sitting on a bench in Heckscher Playground, staring at the same slide where two unsupervised children started a chain of events that has landed me right back in the same spot. Only this time, I'm alone, and the only thing that's unsupervised is my life.

My hands shake as I type out the text I swore I wouldn't send. Twenty-eight days. That's all our pretend engagement was supposed to last in their eyes. For four weeks, Niall and I met at this same spot and built something that neither of us expected or wanted.

One promise unfulfilled.

Staring at the ring that's still on my hand, I give it a twirl and hit send.

So, I'm here at the park. Obviously, you're not. It's 2:00 p.m. on Sunday, and I'm banking on the fact that you're a creature of habit. Don't let me down.

4:00 p.m.

Two hours. Wow. You sure like to make a grand entrance, huh?

6:00 p.m.

Okay, if you insist. I forgive you.

Yeah, that one is a stretch. I admit it.

Waiting for him is hopeless. I knew that the minute I sat down. But four hours later, here I am, watching every person who walks by, praying that by some twist of fate he decides to forgive me and shows up for our standing Sunday date at Central Park.

I shouldn't be shocked I'm alone. It's not like he's given me anything but radio silence since last night.

I don't know what I'd hoped for. Maybe a Hail Mary? An olive branch? A miracle? I feel like screaming while pulling my hair out and then crying until I give up. A stabbing pain radiates from my chest as I glance down at my phone again, my hope fading as I send one last text.

I still have your ring. If you won't talk to me, at least give Vince my number so I can arrange for him to return it to you safely.

7:30 p.m.

For what it's worth, despite everything, I fell in love with chocolate ice cream. More than you'll ever know.

One of my favorite movies is *Never Been Kissed*. It's one of those "come from behind" chick flicks where the heroine has a secret hidden agenda the whole movie. She goes undercover and pretends to be a high school student to get the digs on a teacher who has the hots for her. Gross, right? Only she ends up falling for him and fucks it all up.

Kind of like I did. Except after the heroine's disastrous reveal, the hero realizes he's in love with her and *blah, blah, blah*, her heart was truly in the right place. He shows up at the very last minute, right as all seems lost, and sweeps her into a passionate kiss while someone starts a slow clap in the background, and everything ends with some uplifting music.

Well, reality check. Real life is no rom com, and there's no happily ever after for me.

As I pack up, I lift my hand, letting the sun sparkle through the brilliant stone on my hand one more time before I slip it off. Life doesn't end up like it does in the movies.

No matter how hard you try to do the right thing.

We are pleased to offer you an internship with Trask & Payne Enterprises. We are impressed with your skills and are confident your qualifications are well-suited to our immediate needs. Enclosed you will find a Trask & Payne welcome packet as well as information pertaining to your start date and division assignment. Welcome aboard.

I could say that two weeks later, I held the sixth letter from Trask and Payne in my hands—the golden ticket, the *one*—and it's as sweet as I imagined it'd be.

I could say that, but I'd be a fucking liar.

It's bittersweet. I don't feel the euphoria of finally landing the job of my dreams. Maybe because it cost me everything. Yes, I managed to secure the internship on my own, and I guess that's something to be proud of. However, I'll never be proud of the pain I caused, and especially the look of disappointment in Niall's eyes. I'll never recover from that for as long as I live.

Getting dressed for my first day on the job should be monumental. It should be like the first day of high school, where you can hardly sleep. Where you get up way before the alarm clock goes off, just so you can pick out the perfect outfit to start the final leg of your adolescence. Instead, I slept through my alarm, barely made it in the shower, and pulled out the least wrinkled business suit I could find from my closet.

Grabbing a disposable coffee cup, I fill it to the rim and make my way toward my new office building when my phone rings. My heart skips a beat, and for a moment I pretend it's Niall calling to forgive me for everything. But the minute I glance at the caller ID, my stomach falls to my feet and that one spark of hope returns to a black void.

Keeping my head down, I make my way toward Madison Avenue and answer with a forced a cheerfulness I don't feel. "Are you ready to jump ship and come be my assistant?"

"Funny, girl. You *are* an assistant."

"That shows how much you know. Assistants can have assistants these days. Welcome to the new corporate America."

Lollie laughs as I weave my way through the throngs of pedestrians on their way to work in midtown Manhattan. "I just called to wish you luck. How does it feel to finally get everything you've ever wanted in life?"

"Not at all like I expected."

"I know," she says quietly. After spilling my guts to her about the disaster which shall not be named, Lollie and I came an understanding. I don't speak of it and neither does she. It's better that way. I need to move on with my life and stay focused. Living in the past and wallowing in a river of what-ifs will only drown me.

"How's my little dude?" I ask, desperate to change the subject.

"Missing you. He still talks about you all the time."

"I miss him too."

After Gloria fired me on the spot, she refused to let me see Preston. Besides Lollie, I was one of the only constants in his life, and it broke my heart to know he thought I'd abandoned him. Luckily, my little chat with Gloria in the park cured that. Although

194

with the demands of my new job, I won't get to see him nearly as often as I'd like. I know what it feels like to be abandoned. I wouldn't wish it on my worst enemy.

"He keeps asking about the wedding, you know."

I rub my forehead, creases wrinkling under my fingers. "Wedding?"

"The one his *mother* announced at the gala. He told me all about it. He says you and Niall are getting married. He's been practicing walking you and Sophie down the aisle in front of all the mirrors in the house."

I should've seen this coming. I should've realized Niall and I tangled two innocent lives in our web of deceit. During our planning and fake courtship, Sophie and Preston had forged a real friendship. Not the fake kind Niall and I forced, but one based on innocence and honesty.

"The ceremony might get a little awkward when the groom doesn't show up." I manage a dry laugh and cross the street to my new office building. "He hasn't returned my calls for weeks, Lollie. It's over.

I blew it."

"I refuse to believe that."

"You're a hopeless romantic, you know that?"

"So are you."

"I used to be, but I've decided that stuff's not for me anymore. I'm over them."

"You're right. I mean, those kind of movie kisses and happily ever afters don't happen in real life. Especially like that dumb kissing scene in *The Notebook*, which is the worst movie of all time."

"Oh my God, shut up!" I yell as I open the door to the massive skyscraper. "*The Notebook* is the greatest love story of all time. That kiss? Holy shit, that's the greatest kiss in movie history, Lollie, what's wrong with you? The thunder? The rain? The boat? Are you kidding me? They're all wet and he tells her it'll never be over. She goes to scream at him, and then he shuts her up with a kiss! No happily ever after trumps a shut-up kiss."

A few beats of silence pass before I hear her smugness through the line. "Told you— hopeless romantic."

Letting out a frustrated scream, I pull the phone away and yell into the mouthpiece. "I'm hanging up on you now."

As I make my way to the elevators, I make a mental note to throw out all my copies of *The Notebook* when I get home.

I'm single-handedly keeping Starbucks in business.

Two weeks into my internship and I think I'm about to break a record for the most hours worked. I'm not kidding. Beyond my classes and homework, I live, eat, and breathe Trask and Payne. I'm the first one in the office on Monday morning and the last one to leave on Friday night. Sometimes Vince and I even work on Saturdays.

Yes, I said Vince. I'm personal assistant to Vincent Tribiotti. Don't get any ideas. We're strictly professional. I know he has a reputation, and trust me, I've seen it in action a few times. However, Vince has been nothing but courteous to me. Maybe it's because he respects me. Maybe it's because I was fake engaged to his best friend for four weeks.

Who knows.

At least he has the decency to never mention Niall, and for the most part, I haven't had to deal with seeing my former betrothed around the office. Usually, Niall's job keeps him on location and in the public eye. Vince and I work behind the scenes on projects, and that's just fine with me. I don't need any reminders of what I lost.

"I need projections for the Halpert account, Laken," Vince says, taking the double espresso I brought for him on my morning coffee run. "I need them bound in a report along with graphs—pie, bar, line, all that shit. I need it all."

My brows rise. "By one o'clock? Are you serious?"

"Come on, Laken. You're resourceful. You can do this. If we're going to save this account, I need you with me." Stopping in the middle of the breakroom hallway, he settles a hand on each of my shoulders and holds my stare. "Are you with me?"

"I'm with you. I'm with you." I nod emphatically while wondering when the hell I'll have time to breathe, much less get all this done before noon.

With ten minutes to spare, I close fifteen folders and pack them up, ready to make Vince shine in the meeting. I've done my job, and hopefully I'll be able to ride his coattails far enough for someone to notice me. Getting noticed is all it takes around here—then you're gold.

I follow Vince into the meeting and take my seat beside him. He gives my hand a pat before standing and addressing the Halpert delegates.

"As you know, we've worked on your account for many years, and while our relationship has always been a mutually beneficial one, we think it's time to shake things up a bit." Moving stealthily from chair to chair, Vince charms everyone, and I smile. For all of his faults, the man can work a room like nobody's business.

"Shake things up how?" a Halpert

representative asks.

"I'm glad you asked, Joel." Vince throws his hands out and mimics a big screen. "I'm thinking a larger scale marketing campaign like no one has ever seen before. With the help of my amazing assistant," he lays a heavy hand on my shoulder, "and artwork by a photographer who will blow you away with his eye for detail, we're going to take the market by storm."

If you've made it this far in the story, you know where this is going, right? I'm glad *you* do, because my dumb ass just sits there grinning like a cat on Quaaludes while Vince works his magic.

I thought I'd turned a corner, but shit never goes like it's supposed to go. That's not life, and it sure as hell isn't mine. Know why? Because karma is a bitch, and she's dressed in thigh high fuck-me boots as she walks tall and proud behind *him*. The man who strolls into the meeting five minutes late and flips my world upside down.

"Sorry I'm late, everyone. I had to drop my daughter off at school. Traffic was a bleedin' nightmare."

I stop breathing. The visceral reaction from just hearing his voice tears me to shreds. I will myself not to look at him, but my eyes refuse to listen and take him all in. He looks even better than I remember. The navy blue suit he wears hugs him in all the right places, and his crisp white shirt presses against his hard chest as his red power tie dominates the room.

I manage a smile, and he returns it with a scowl. My stomach twists until I realize Vince still has his hand resting on my shoulder, and that's exactly where Niall's eyes are glued. I think about shrugging Vince's hand off, but at least I'm getting some kind of reaction out of Niall, and the heat in his eyes is just too tempting to pass up.

I know I'm walking a fine line here. Smoke and mirrors are exactly what got us into this mess in the first place. However, what do I have to lose?

Smiling, I pat Vince's hand and settle deeper into my seat as the sound of a pencil snapping fills the room. Out of the corner of my eye, I glance over and see Niall tossing the two halves onto the table and then running his hands over his face.

Game on.

Again.

We file out of the conference room with Vince high-fiving every manager and executive at Halpert like it's a pep rally, when I feel a hand grab my elbow.

"Quiet," Niall mumbles in my ear.

I stumble behind him as he drags me down the hallway and through the breakroom, his pace unrelenting and his grip hard. All the color is gone from his eyes, leaving only a dominating black stare. I don't know what I'm in for as he drags me into a cramped supply closet, but by the predatory look on his face, it's not an apology.

I take a step backward and raise my palm in an attempt to ward off his tirade. "Niall, please don't start—"

Slamming the door, he spins me around

and backs me against a wall of shelves stocked with office supplies. As my back crashes into the ledges, our lips clash, and it's not gentle. It's hurried and frantic and about as romantic as you'd think making out in a supply closet would be. But holy fuck, it's hot. Immediately, my hands go to his waistband and jerk his shirt out from the confines of his belt before diving under it and touching his hard chest.

Fuck, I've missed this chest.

I can barely breathe as he kisses me on my lips, my face, my neck, my hair, anything he can reach. His tongue is tasting, and I'm about to lose my mind. My head drops back, and I whimper as Niall groans and pulls my jacket off my shoulders. Unbuttoning the first few buttons on my dress, he jerks the lace of my bra down and trails a heated path from my chin to my breast. The minute his tongue scrapes over my overly-sensitized nipple, I let out a moan that I'm certain can be heard all the way to the breakroom.

This is it. I'm going to die right here in this closet, all because I crave his touch. I'll give up everything for it. Even the one thing I risked it for in the first place. Unable to stop myself, I reach between our bodies and cup him, my blood boiling as his teeth graze the tip of my nipple.

"Turn around and spread ye legs," he commands hotly, pulling back and licking his lips.

Just the sound of his voice almost makes me come on the spot, but I manage to lift my head and stare at him with an open mouth. "We can't. Niall, someone will hear us. I just started this job," I halfway protest, but I'm already curling my fist around the shelf in preparation of his onslaught. "I can't…shit, I can't get fired already."

"I outrank ye arse in this office." He's nearly losing control. In the short time we've been together, I know his accent gets heavier when the desire to fight or fuck overtakes him. "Christ, Laken, just around before someone comes in."

Weeks of missing him and hating myself come crashing down, blinding me to what's right or wrong. All I can see is what's in front of me and the sinful way he's manipulating my body.

I know it's only about to get worse.

Or better.

Hell, I can't even think anymore, but I can listen. Turning around, I grip the shelves and spread my legs. Even in the dim light, I see the wicked grin tipping the corners of Niall's mouth from over my shoulder. After bunching my skirt around my waist, he lowers his zipper and then crowds in behind me, his rigid length settling between my ass cheeks.

"Were ye trying to make me jealous today, Laken?"

My world is spinning as I feel him grab hold of the base of his cock. Moving my panties to the side, he slides it between my slick folds. "No," I groan, leaning my forehead against the shelf for support.

He pushes the tip in just enough to drive me insane. "No?"

"Niall…"

His hands reach around me from behind and squeeze my breasts, and I push my ass backward in an attempt to force him inside me. I whimper at the loss when he pulls back out.

"I'll ask again. Were ye trying to make me feckin' jealous of my own friend today?"

"Yes! Fine, all right? Is that what you want to hear? You've frozen me out for the last three weeks, Niall! I wanted your attention."

"Well, ye have it now. Ye want to talk… let's talk." He slams into me, only stilling for a moment before sliding back out and then driving back in.

I welcome his punishing pace, because at the end of the day, I know I deserve it. It's what I need to rid myself of this guilt. Maybe this is what will finally allow me to sleep at night.

One final fuck. The nail in the coffin.

But one fuck will never be enough with Niall. The heat and sensations between us will only make me crave him more. I know it as sure as I know my own name. Despite the forgiveness I crave, I have to tell him. Even if he tells me to go to hell.

"Niall, I—" But I'm cut off as he fists the back of my hair and pulls my head against his shoulder, continuing to thrust into me with a furious pace. Stars rain down behind my eyelids as I clench hard around him and spasm, exploding into a chorus of curses and cries of his name.

With two more punishing drives into my body, he lowers his lips to my ear, groaning in a ragged voice as he comes deep inside me. "Mother, student, nanny, intern...I don't give a feckin' hell who ye are. No one will ever love ye the way I love ye. Do ye hear me? No one."

Niall releases my hair, and with the smell of sex surrounding us, everything becomes deathly silent in the tiny closet. Biting my lip, I think of all the things I should say as he zips up his pants, but before I can get a word out, he punches the shelf and lets out a string of curses before slamming the door on his way out.

I'm alone in a darkened supply closet with only my shame to keep me company. Only, I have none. That guilt I should feel for screwing a fellow employee at work? Yeah, that piece of conscience is waiting outside with earplugs.

And that tiny spark of hope? The one that struggled to stay lit when I saw him walk into that meeting? It's now a burning inferno, and any thoughts I had of walking away from Niall Mackay have been shot to hell with the admission I know he never meant to voice.

He loves me.

Chapter Eleven
NIALL

I stare at the text moments after I type it. Seeing her wasn't on my agenda for the day. Fucking her in a closet definitely wasn't. But walking out on her afterward was the worst offense of all.

I'm such a feckin' idiot.

She won't listen, even if I try to explain why I did it. No one in their right mind would.

I just hope I can make her listen in a language she'll understand.

To make this look good, we should get to know each other a little better. What do you say we go out, just the two of us? No kids.

I press send and hope she'll show.

I've barely been at the park ten minutes when I see her.

Showtime.

Pulling out the iconic diamond pendant with the sapphire stone, I climb on the park bench and pump my fists in the air. "Having my daughter kick the shite out of the boy ye were paid to watch, was the best thing that ever happened to me. It brought me to ye. Don't give up. No matter what happens, promise me ye won't ever give up on me."

"Niall, what are you doing?" Laken asks, her fists clenched by her side.

"Movie." I pause mid-theatrics. "I need the name of the movie."

"You somewhat quoted *Titanic*. Again, what the hell are you doing? Get down from there! People are staring."

Pulling the poignant teddy bear from the bag I left on the bench, I cross the few remaining steps between us and drop the necklace and the bear in her hand. "This is what I'm doing. All the insignificant things we've done together, ye think they're nothing at the time, but when ye add all that shite up? They mean we're supposed to be together. The first time I saw ye, touched ye, kissed ye, it was like coming home."

A small smile teases the corners of her mouth. "That was almost *Sleepless in Seattle*."

Snapping my fingers, I make the signal, and Laken lets out a blood curdling scream as Vince tosses two buckets of water on us, drenching both of us from head to toe.

"Niall! What the actual fuck?"

Grabbing her by the shoulders, I pull her into me. "This is going to be hard as feckin' hell. I'll probably screw up most every day, but I'm willing to screw up because I want ye. All of ye, forever. Every day. Every single feckin' day."

Tears run down her face, disappearing into her already drenched shirt. "Oh God, did you just absolutely destroy my favorite quote from *The Notebook*?" A small laugh escapes as she tries to cover her mouth.

"Completely." I'm winning her over, and I haven't even gotten to my Hail Mary yet.

"Are you done?" she asks, trying to look

serious.

I give her a wink. "Almost."

Backing up, I stand on the bench again and clear my throat, belting out *The Way You Look Tonight* in the most off-key singing voice ever heard in public. Children stop playing, adults come to a complete stand-still, and everyone stares as I finish the last few lines and take a deep breath. Thunderous applause erupts, and after a few bows to my adoring public, I climb off the bench and wait for a reaction.

She lets out a long breath, still obviously in shock. "Wow."

"I've never sung in public before," I admit.

"I can see why."

Holding her eye, I finish my speech from the nine-hour rom com marathon I watched in preparation for this moment. "Tell me ye love me. Say it out loud. Say it right now before it's too late. Because in this park, I'm just a photographer asking an ex-nanny to love me."

"You just did a *My Best Friend's Wedding-*

212

Notting Hill bastard hybrid."

"I'm going for extra credit."

"We need to talk." Sighing, she sits on the bench and fidgets with the ring on her finger. My ring. She's still wearing it.

Mainly because I'd refused her calls when she tried to return it.

Although I know she's right, and I'm the one who asked her to meet me here, the phrase "we need to talk" evokes dread inside of me. Nothing good ever comes from those four words.

I sit down. "I know."

"I miss you."

"I miss ye too." And I do. I miss her so much I can't feckin' sleep at night because I know I'll dream of her. I have a hard time getting dressed for work in the morning because every time I do, all I remember is the way her knees buckled in the supply closet. But mostly, I can't turn on the television because undoubtedly, there's some feckin' rom com movie on and all I can think is, *I bet Laken has seen this one.*

It's maddening.

"The job's going well?"

She nods and smiles. "Vince is a little hard to handle."

"Vince is a pushover," I answer. Sighing, I palm the back of my neck in realization that my grand attempt at winning her back failed miserably. "All ye need to do is field calls from his conquests who can't take a hint and ye will be in his debt forever. But if ye tell him I said that, I'll deny it."

Her fingers play with the fur on the teddy bear. "Duly noted."

I can't stand it anymore. I have to break this monotonous chitchat. "Laken, I'm sorry for walking out of the supply closet. I'm sorry for ignoring ye calls after the gala. We have a lot to work on, but I'm willing, if ye are. Our story may have begun as a lie, but it doesn't have to end as one."

"Do you forgive me," she asks tilting her chin as she squints into the sun.

I don't even have to think. "There's nothing to forgive, Laken. I overreacted out of shock. I'm Irish. Cut me some slack."

Clipping the sapphire necklace around

her nape, she glances up with a dramatic sigh. "What are you doing for dinner?"

"I'm busy," I say, managing a deadpan stare without an ounce of enthusiasm.

Laken's face falls, and she grips the bear closer to her body as she stands. "Oh."

Without hesitation, I grab her and crush her against my chest. Pressing our lips together, I deliver a kiss that can make all her rom com movies go feck themselves. "What are ye doing for breakfast?"

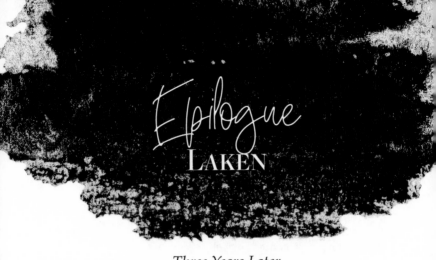

Epilogue
LAKEN

Three Years Later

As the last coat of Blue Mermaid Shimmer #9 dries on Sophie's fingers, I help her into her silver sequined spaghetti strapped dress and pull her long dark hair into a stylish loose bun on top of her head.

"This is my favorite color," she says, holding her hand out and fanning it in the air. "I used to paint my own nails this same shade when I was a little girl."

I can't help but chuckle. "You're only eleven, Soph. You're still a little girl." She looks at our reflections in the mirror and raises an eyebrow at me, the rebellious girl she once was still floating underneath the surface of tulle and lace. "There." Clipping

216

the last of the crystals in her hair, I stand and hand her a mirror. "All done."

Sophie turns around and inspects the back of her hair, nodding in approval. "It's nice to have someone fix my hair the right way for a change. Dad used to make me look like I needed medication." Popping up from the chair, she gives me a quick peck on the cheek. "Thanks, Mom."

Mom.

It still slams my heart every time she says it.

Bounding out of the room, she almost makes it to the door when she's blocked by a six-foot-two powerhouse of a man dressed in a black suit jacket, white dress shirt, and a baby blue tie that matches Sophie's nails. Anyone glancing at him would mistake him for the corporate executive he'd become.

Then the image is ruined by his dusty beard and unkempt "don't care" hair. The strands twist every which way as if he'd run his hands through it and paced the floor in preparation for tonight.

But the part that has me almost doubled

over in laughter is the Scottish kilt he's wearing in place of pants.

Sophie's eyes widen in horror. "Dad! Oh my God, no! Just no. You cannot wear that thing to the father-daughter dance at my school."

Niall feigns ignorance, tilting his head while running a finger down his tie. "And why not? Does something not match?"

"Yeah, your skirt. Dad, you're wearing a skirt! Where are your pants?"

"Soph, it's called a kilt. It's Scottish."

"You're Irish."

"Aye, but ye great-grandmother isn't. She's full-blooded Scottish, and I thought this would be a great opportunity to show off ye heritage to ye friends at school."

Sophie turns to me in a panic, her arms waving frantically. "Mom! Do something!"

I shrug. "I kind of like it." Pinching his side, I whisper, "Leave it on for later."

"I love feckin' with her," he whispers with a low laugh as he rakes his heated eyes down my body. "Later, huh? Ye didn't get enough of it last night?"

Sophie makes a face and walks away grumbling. "Gross."

"Hey, I'm seven months pregnant, buddy." I gesture to my round frame. "I take easy access where I can get it."

"Ye are insatiable, Mrs. Mackay." A concerned look crosses his face as he wraps an arm around my waist and pulls me to him. "Did ye tell Vince ye are quitting at the end of the week?"

"Um…"

"Laken…" he groans impatiently. "We talked about this. Ye need to take some time off before the baby comes. Ye have been pushing yourself too hard since ye promotion. Lollie can handle shite until ye come back."

I know he's right. In the last year, Vince Tribiotti was promoted to senior account executive, and I'd acquired his job as project manager. In the interim, I'd finagled Lollie an interview as my assistant and she blew it out of the water. Honestly, she exceeded all my expectations. I had no idea the woman possessed such a killer business instinct.

However, with the way she'd trapped Gloria with the security tapes without batting an eye, I shouldn't have been shocked. Still, even a couple months away from giving birth, I'm hesitant to leave my position, even if it's just for a few months of maternity leave.

Niall runs a hand across my stomach. "Have ye called Preston to tell him yet?"

"No, I thought we could do it together when we take the kids ice skating this weekend."

"What do ye think of your name, Miss Presley Paige Mackay? Think ye namesake will share it with ye?" Our daughter rewards him with a strong kick against his hand.

"So, my friends and I want to go to a diner after the dance," Sophie interrupts, wedging her way between us. "You guys don't have a problem with that, do you?"

Niall's mouth tightens into a hard line. "Sophie, ye are only eleven. This is New York City. Ye can't just run around unsupervised."

Thinking back to a warm spring day three years ago, I can't help but grin. "Hmmm, that sounds a little familiar. Do you have that on an index card of go-to comebacks?"

"Watch it," he says, jabbing a finger my way before pulling me closer.

Weaving one hand around his neck, I straighten his already impeccably straight tie with the other. "If she wasn't unsupervised, we would've never met."

"Are ye trying to say we're married because of my shite parenting skills?"

I shrug. "If the father figure fits…"

Wrapping his hand around me, he pulls me in close and brushes his lips over mine. With a few more insistent yet tasteful kisses, he leans back and stares at me, the corners of his eyes lighting up as he brushes his thumbs across my cheeks.

"Gross," Sophie repeats, tapping her brand-new heels while standing by the door.

Giving her a side-eye glance, Niall laughs and returns his smile toward me, brushing a finger against the tip of my nose. "I guess I finally made an honest woman out of ye."

I raise an eyebrow at him and wait for

the punchline.

Running a hand over my swollen belly again, he whispers in my ear. "I made ye a mom after all."

"No," I say, stealing a look at my impatient, beautiful daughter as Niall reaches for his camera to immortalize the moment. "You made me a family."

"If you two are finished kissing, can we go to my dance, please?" Opening the door to our new apartment, Sophie stands in the hallway as Niall kisses me one last time before reaching behind the cushion of the couch and pulling out a canvas bag full of DVDs.

Curious, I dive through the contents. "*Pretty in Pink*? *27 Dresses*, *How to Lose A Guy In Ten Days*? What is this, some kind of trick?"

"What's this?" Niall's eyes widen and he shakes his head. "Woman, what kind of rom com enthusiast are ye? They're all the movies on ye must-see list. Since Soph and I are leaving ye alone for the night, I thought ye could pick two or three, and I promise to watch them without argument." With a grin, my husband turns and escorts his daughter to her first dance.

As the door closes behind, I flip through the movies one more time, then dump the entire contents in the trashcan and close the lid.

I heard that gasp.

Here's the thing about rom coms— they're the adult version of fairytales, feeding the ideal that we all have that one soulmate out there. Even though they all take on different versions, the ugly truth is that we all buy into it. We watch them, even though there's that little piece inside of us that knows there's little to no chance of ever finding a love like the ones we see in the movies. What guy in their right mind would be willing to wait years for us like Noah in *The Notebook*? So why even try? What makes us continue to believe that men like that really exist?

I'll tell you why.

Because they do.

I found my Noah. And my Jack. And my

Edward. And my Michael. And my William. And even my creepy Mr. Coulson. He kissed me in the rain. He went down with the ship for me. He got me the job and the apartment. He sang to me. He asked me to love him. And he forgave me for pretending to be someone I wasn't.

Rom coms are a dime a dozen. Two hours of your life, and they're over. But Niall Mackay? He's one in a million.

And my story? It's not a fairytale.

It's forever.

Acknowledgments

K.A., there aren't enough thank yous for what you do for me every day. If it weren't for you, I'd still be perched up on that ledge, teetering over the edge. Thanks for being the only one who can tame the crazy.

Crystal, thank you for your endless support for the Irish, Scottish, Australian—and that one time I made him slightly Canadian—Niall. Your encouragement is everything and I simply couldn't function without you.

To my speed queen beta readers, Crystal, Trish, Sara, Angie, Meagan, Heather, Misty, and Tami….the next rom com fest is on me!

Trish, thank you for making Niall sound authentic. You are my Irish goddess. I owe you a pint of the black stuff!

Thanks to Arien Johnston and Jamie McBride for winning my frantic "name my character" contest. It's because of you two that

Laken Cavanaugh exists!

Cora's Twisted Alpha Addicts and Cora's Dark Angels, you keep me sane, you keep me laughing, and your pimpin' skills are legendary. I love your faces.

Gillian Leonard, thanks for being an amazing editor and for continually being there. I'll always count you as one of the *good* things I got out of "that" deal.

Lastly, thanks to the readers and bloggers who share this story. Without you, my vision just stays with me. You help it grow. Thank you for all you do for our community.

About the Author

Cora Kenborn is a *USA Today* bestselling author who writes everything from dark and twisted mafia romances to laugh-out-loud romcoms. Known for her damaged bad boys and feisty heroines, Cora promises her readers a happily ever after, although she'll take them on an emotional roller coaster before handing it over.

Cora fully admits to having the eating habits of a toddler and regularly sneaks oversized bag of gummy bears and various forms of caffeine into her office because adulting is hard. Since the domestic Southern Belle gene apparently skips a generation, she spends most of her free time convincing her family that microwaving Hot Pockets counts as cooking dinner.

Oh, and autocorrect thinks she's obsessed with ducks.

Find Cora Online

Newsletter
Website
Bookbub
Facebook
Cora's Twisted Alpha Addicts Reader Group
Twitter
Instagram
Goodreads
Spotify

Also by
CORA KENBORN

Carrera Cartel Trilogy
Blurred Red Lines
Faded Gray Lines
Drawn Blue Lines

Lords of Lyre Duet
Fame and Obsession
Fame and Secrets

Standalones
Cursed In Love
Darkest Deeds
Shallow
Unsupervised
Blacklisted (Craving: Bad Anthology)
Starlet (*coming soon*)

Swamp Bottom Novella Series
Front Porches and Funerals

Voodoo and Vodka
Hook-ups and Hang-ups
Blue Lights and Boatmen
Pink Lines and Panic
Divorce and Denial
Warrants and Onesies

Made in United States
North Haven, CT
30 January 2022

15430981R00145